KU-714-775

The Hardy Boys
in
What Happened at Midnight

Hardy Boys® Mystery Stories in Armada

1 The Mystery of the Aztec Warrior
2 The Arctic Patrol Mystery
3 The Haunted Fort
4 The Mystery of the Whale Tattoo
5 The Mystery of the Disappearing Floor
6 The Mystery of the Desert Giant
7 The Mystery of the Melted Coins
8 The Mystery of the Spiral Bridge
9 The Clue of the Screeching Owl
10 While the Clock Ticked
11 The Twisted Claw
12 The Wailing Siren Mystery
13 The Secret of the Caves
14 The Secret of Pirates' Hill
15 The Flickering Torch Mystery
16 The Secret of the Old Mill
17 The Shore Road Mystery
18 The Great Airport Mystery
19 The Sign of the Crooked Arrow
20 The Clue in the Embers
21 What Happened at Midnight
22 The Sinister Signpost
23 Footprints Under the Window
24 The Crisscross Shadow
25 Hunting for Hidden Gold
26 The Mystery of Cabin Island
27 The Mark on the Door
28 The Yellow Feather Mystery
29 The Hooded Hawk Mystery
30 The Secret Agent on Flight 101
31 The Tower Treasure
32 The Mystery of the Missing Friends
33 The Viking Symbol Mystery
34 The Mystery of the Chinese Junk
35 The Mystery at Devil's Paw
36 The Ghost at Skeleton Rock
37 The Clue of the Broken Blade
38 The Secret of Wildcat Swamp
39 The Phantom Freighter
40 The Secret of Skull Mountain
41 The Mysterious Caravan
42 Danger on Vampire Trail
43 The Bombay Boomerang
44 The Masked Monkey
45 The Shattered Helmet
46 The Clue of the Hissing Serpent
47 The Jungle Pyramid
48 The Firebird Rocket
*
57 Night of the Werewolf
58 The Mystery of the Samurai Sword
59 The Pentagon Spy
60 The Apeman's Secret
61 The Mummy Case
62 The Mystery of Smugglers Cove
63 The Stone Idol
64 The Vanishing Thieves
65 The Outlaw's Silver
66 The Submarine Caper
67 The Four-Headed Dragon
68 The Infinity Clue
69 Track of the Zombie
70 The Voodoo Plot
71 The Billion Dollar Ransom
72 The Tic-Tac Terror
73 Trapped at Sea
74 Game Plan for Disaster
75 The Crimson Flame
76 Cave-In
77 Sky Sabotage
78 The Roaring River Mystery
79 The Demon's Den
80 The Blackwing Puzzle
81 The Swamp Monster
82 Revenge of the Desert Phantom
83 The Skyfire Puzzle

For contractual reasons, Armada has been obliged to publish from No. 57 onwards before publishing Nos. 49–56. These missing numbers will be published as soon as possible.

The Hardy Boys® Mystery Stories

What Happened at Midnight

Franklin W. Dixon

ARMADA

First published in the U.K. in 1972 by
William Collins Sons & Co. Ltd, London and Glasgow
First published in Armada in 1975
This impression 1990

Armada is an imprint of
the Children's Division, part of
the Collins Publishing Group,
8 Grafton Street, London W1X 3LA

Printed and bound in Great Britain by
William Collins Sons & Co. Ltd, Glasgow

Frank brought the man down with a flying tackle

CONTENTS

CHAPTER		PAGE
1	BURGLARS	9
2	AMAZING INVENTION	18
3	WARNING MESSAGE	23
4	THE COLD TRAIL	32
5	THE HUNT	41
6	FOGGED IN	51
7	THE ESCAPE	59
8	AN ASTOUNDING REPORT	67
9	SMUGGLER'S TRAIL	74
10	ELEVATOR CHASE	80
11	DISCOVERED!	86
12	TUNNEL SCARE	92
13	EXCITING ASSIGNMENT	100
14	IDENTIFICATION DIAMOND	107
15	PURSUIT	115
16	BAIL OUT!	120
17	THE TRAPPED PILOT	125
18	OUTSMARTING THE ENEMY	134
19	ANCHOR PETE	142
20	CAPTIVES' HIDEOUT	149

·1·

Burglars

"WHAT an assignment! And from our own Dad!"

Joe Hardy grinned at his brother Frank as the two boys slipped into ripple soled shoes and put on dark jackets.

"First time we've ever been asked to play burglar," Frank answered with a chuckle.

A few days before, their father, an ace detective, and Malcolm Wright, an inventor, had left for California to hunt for Wright's valuable stolen antique plane. Because they would be delayed in returning, the inventor had requested the brothers to "break into" his home and retrieve a top-secret invention before thieves took it.

"A little nefarious work around midnight," Joe mused, "and all because Mr Wright left his keys inside the house and locked everything but one bedroom window with a broken lock."

"The invention must be something super or Dad and Mr Wright wouldn't have asked us to guard it with our lives," Frank remarked. "I wonder what it is."

"Dad gave us permission to find out. Say, suppose we can't locate that secret compartment we think is in Mr Wright's desk before those thieves arrive?" Joe

9

asked. "I wish Dad could have given us all the details before the call was cut off and we couldn't get it back."

Joe, who had blond hair, was a year younger than his dark-haired, eighteen-year-old brother Frank. Both had solved many mysteries, some of them for their father.

Fenton Hardy had told the boys on the telephone that just before Mr Wright had left Bayport, where they all lived, he had been threatened by a mysterious gang. They had learned about the invention from a worker in a factory that had made some of the parts. He had breached the confidence placed in him.

The caller had told Mr Wright that if he did not voluntarily turn over his invention before a certain time, "visitors" would come for it. The date they had set was the following day!

"Mr Wright didn't have time to put the invention in a safe-deposit box, so he hid it in his study," Fenton Hardy had said. "He's afraid the thieves may break into his house, so he has alerted the police to be there tomorrow morning. But he's worried and he wants you boys to get the small box containing the invention before then. Don't leave it at our house when you're not there. Keep it with you at all times but well hidden."

Frank and Joe relayed the conversation to their pretty, understanding mother, and to Aunt Gertrude, their father's maiden sister who lived with them. She was inclined to be critical of her nephews' involvement in detective work.

Instantly she said, "Be burglars! The idea! Why, suppose you fall off that house—!"

"Gertrude, *please!*" Mrs Hardy broke in. "Don't even mention such a possibility. I know the boys will be careful."

"Of course," said Joe. "Let's go, Frank!"

The brothers hurried to the garage where their shiny convertible gleamed in the light of a street lamp on the corner of High and Elm streets. Frank took the wheel and drove to within a block of Mr Wright's rambling, old-fashioned house. The boys walked to it and were glad to see that the building stood in deep shadows.

They reconnoitred the grounds in silence. No one was about. Finally Frank whispered, "I guess our best bet to the upper story is that trellis. It looks sturdy. We'll go across the roof over the kitchen door and edge round to the unlocked window."

"I'll stay close by and hold on to your legs until you make it," Joe answered.

They followed each other up the trellis and crossed the narrow roof. Fortunately there was not much pitch to it. Joe crouched and grasped his brother's right leg.

"All set," he announced in a whisper.

Frank stretched over to the window ledge but could not reach the top of the sash to raise it.

"Give me a push up," he murmured to Joe, who hoisted his brother until his fingers reached the top of the sash.

The window lifted easily. Frank pulled himself sideways through it. "Your turn, Joe." He reached out and grasped his brother's outstretched hands.

Joe, a little shorter than Frank, found he could not reach the window without swinging precariously in space. If Frank couldn't hold his brother's weight, he

would be dragged outside. Both boys would plunge to
the ground!

"No use being silly about this," Frank said. "I'll open
the rear door for you."

Joe was about to climb down the trellis when a
strong light suddenly lit the area.

"A car!" Frank exclaimed as the driver beamed a
searchlight on their side of the street. "Maybe the
thieves are in it! Duck!"

Frank quickly closed the window, while Joe flattened
himself face down on the roof. He did not stand up until
the area was in darkness again. Then he hurried down
the trellis and through the rear door.

"Close call!" said Frank.

Joe nodded. "I thought maybe it was a police car,
but I guess not. It had no revolving top light."

His brother agreed. "I'm sure Mr Wright's enemies
are casing this place!"

"Yes. And they'll probably be back soon! We'd
better get moving."

Holding their flashlights low to the floor, the boys
sped up the stairs and found Mr Wright's study. A
large walnut desk stood in the centre of the room. Frank
and Joe walked to the front of it, where there were
drawers to left and right of the wide kneehole.

"The secret compartment may be in one of them,"
Joe suggested.

"They're not locked," Frank whispered in amaze-
ment.

The boys searched diligently, lifting aside letters and
other papers. They found nothing.

"Now what?" Joe asked.

"A car!" Frank exclaimed. "Maybe the thieves are in it!"

Frank had an idea. "I'll look in the kneehole while you hunt for movable panels on the outside of the desk."

Again there was silence as the two boys began to finger the woodwork. Minutes went by, then Joe said, "I've found something that moves."

Frank crawled out and watched as his brother slid open a panel, revealing a long, narrow space.

"Anything in it?" Frank asked.

Joe beamed his flashlight inside. A look of disappointment came over his face.

"Nothing," he announced. "There might have been at some time, though."

"You mean the invention?"

"Maybe. How are you making out?"

"Something in the kneehole looks suspicious," Frank answered.

Just then the boys heard the crash of glass and immediately clicked off their flashlights. Someone had broken a windowpane, and at this moment was no doubt reaching inside for the lock. Any minute one or more men might mount the stairs and enter the study!

The boys looked for a hiding place. There were no draperies, sofa, or large chairs, and no cupboard.

"Let's hide in the kneehole," Frank whispered, "then use our hand signals."

Some time before this, the Hardys had devised a series of hand-squeeze signals. One hard squeeze meant, "Let's attack!" Two indicated caution. Long, short, long meant, "We'd better scram." An ordinary handshake was, "Agreed".

"If there are not more than two men, let's attack," Joe said in a barely audible tone.

"Okay.".

Quickly the two crawled into the kneehole and pulled the desk chair into place. The boys were well hidden when they heard footsteps on the stairs, then voices.

"No failing this time or Shorty'll take us on our last ride," said a man with a nasal voice.

Frank and Joe wondered if the men had tried to break in earlier but failed.

The man's companion spoke in lower tones of disgust. "Oh, you'd believe Shorty invented fire if he told you he did. He ain't so great. Takes orders from the boss, don't he?" The other did not reply.

The two men entered the room and beamed flash-lights around. "Where did Wright say he kept the invention?" the deep-toned man asked.

"I got in late on the conversation when I tapped that telephone call to the Hardy house," the other answered. "But I did hear the words 'secret compartment'. Where would that be? The desk?"

Frank and Joe froze. Were they about to be discovered?

"No, not the desk," the other man said. "The safe."

For the first time the boys noticed a small safe standing against the wall opposite them. Frank and Joe were fearful the men would detect their hiding place, but the attention of the burglars was focused on the safe. In a moment they squatted and the boys got a good glimpse of their faces. Both were swarthy and hard-looking.

At that moment the tower clock of the town hall began to strike. It was midnight!

The men waited until the echo of the twelfth stroke had died away, then the one with the nasal twang put his ear to the dial of the safe and began to turn the knob.

After a few moments his companion asked impatiently, "What's the matter? That safecrackin' ear of yours turned to tin?"

"Tumblers are noiseless," the other said. "Guess we'll have to blow it." He began to take some wire from his pocket.

Frank and Joe were trapped. If the door of the safe were blown off, it might head right in their direction!

Quickly Joe felt for Frank's hand and gave it a hard squeeze, meaning, "Let's attack!"

Instantly Frank answered with the "Agreed!" handshake.

In a flash Joe flung the desk chair at the two men, then the boys jumped them!

·2·

Amazing Invention

TAKEN by surprise the burglars were at a disadvantage. Frank and Joe knocked them to the floor and sat on their backs.

"Ugh! What's going—?" one mumbled.

The men were strong and with great heaves they tried to shake off the boys. Frank and Joe pressed down hard.

"Who are you?" Frank demanded.

No answer. Then suddenly the man Joe was holding rolled over and tried to sit up. Joe kept him down and the two, locked in a vice-like grip, twisted to and fro across the floor.

Frank, meanwhile, had found his deep-voiced opponent a kicker, who viciously jabbed his heels into the boy's back. Angry, Frank sent two swift blows which grazed the man's chin.

The other two fighters bumped into them. In the mix-up the burglars were able to throw off their attackers and scramble to their feet. The four began to exchange punches.

"Finish off these guys!" the nasal-voiced man rasped.

For several seconds it looked as if they would. Their blows were swift and well-aimed. Then both men, breathing heavily, relaxed their guard. In a flash Frank and Joe delivered stinging uppercuts to their opponents' jaws. The burglars fell to the floor with thuds that shook the house. They lay quiet.

The boys grinned at each other and Joe said, "Knockouts!"

Frank nodded. "We must notify the police to get out here before these men come to."

"We can wait," Joe answered. "They'll sleep for at least half an hour. Let's find that invention first!"

"Good idea."

Though bruised and weary the boys eagerly searched the side of the kneehole where Frank thought he had found a clue. There was a slight bulge in the wood. After pressing it in several directions, a panel began to slide counter-clockwise. There was a click.

Just then one of the burglars groaned. The Hardys tensed. Was the man coming to? Joe leaned forward and beamed his flashlight on the two figures. Both were still unconscious.

Meanwhile, Frank had lifted out the panel. The space behind it contained a small metal box. Written on the box was: *Property of Malcolm Wright. Valuable. Reward for return.*

"I've found it!" Frank exclaimed.

"Then let's go!" Joe urged.

"Okay," Frank agreed. "You'll find a phone in the lower hall. Call the police while I slip this panel back. Take the box."

In a minute Joe was dialling headquarters. Without giving his name, he said, "Come to Malcolm Wright's house at once. There are burglars in it." He hung up.

Frank joined him and the boys dashed out of the rear door. They took a circuitous route to their convertible to avoid being questioned by the police. At an intersection they saw a police car apparently speeding to the inventor's house.

"Where do you suppose the burglars' car is?" Joe asked. "You'd think they'd have a lookout."

"Maybe it's cruising," Frank suggested.

The boys hopped into their convertible. As an extra precaution against a holdup and possible loss of Mr Wright's invention, they locked themselves in.

"Boy, a lot can happen in an hour," Joe said, looking at the car clock. He reached over and turned on their two-way radio to police headquarters. "I wonder if there's any news yet from the Wright house."

The boys were just in time to pick up a broadcast. An officer was saying, "Send the ambulance to Wright's house."

"Ambulance?" Frank echoed. "Joe, we didn't hit 'em that hard—or did we?"

The policeman went on, "These guys aren't too bad, but they sure got knocked out. Looks like a gang feud. The men who hit them may have done the stealing."

Frank and Joe chuckled. "Some day we'll tell Chief Collig," Frank said, "but right now—"

He stopped speaking as a loud crack of static burst from the radio and a vivid flash of lightning made the night turn to day momentarily. A long roll of thunder followed.

"Looks as if we're in for a bad storm," Joe commented, and Frank put on speed.

A few minutes later the car was parked in the Hardys'

garage. They were mounting the steps of the back porch when the storm broke. Quickly Frank inserted his key in the kitchen door and turned the knob. At once the burglar alarm rang loudly and all the ground floor lights went on.

Joe chuckled. "That'll bring Mother and Aunt Gertrude down in a hurry." He flicked off the alarm.

"And bring the police, too," Frank added. He picked up the kitchen phone and dialled headquarters. "This is Frank Hardy. Our alarm went off by accident. Forget it."

"Okay. You sure everything's all right?" the desk sergeant asked.

"Yes. Thank you. Good night."

By this time the two women had appeared and Mrs Hardy said, "I didn't know the alarm was turned on."

"Well, I did," Aunt Gertrude spoke up. "I wanted to be sure to wake up and see how you boys made out. You must be starved. I'll fix some cocoa and cut slices of cake while you tell—Frank, look at your clothes! Your jacket's torn. And you, Joe, where did you get that lump on your forehead? And your faces—the two of you look as if you've been rolling in the dirt."

"We have." Joe grinned. "Had a big fight. But we saved this!" He pulled the box from his pocket.

As the boys related their adventure, crashing thunder lent a booming orchestration to the story.

"This is the worst storm we've had in years," Mrs Hardy remarked. "I'm glad you boys didn't have to be out in it." When Frank and Joe finished eating, she added, "And now you must get a good night's sleep."

"But first I'd like to open Mr Wright's box and see

just what we have to guard so carefully," Frank said.

Everyone watched excitedly as Joe unwrapped the package. Inside was a small transistor radio.

"Is that all it is?" Aunt Gertrude burst out. "You risked your lives to get *that*?"

The boys were puzzled. Surely their father would not have made such a request if this invention were not unusually valuable.

"Let's turn it on," Frank suggested.

Joe clicked the switch. A man was speaking in Spanish from Madrid, Spain, and announcing the start of a newscast. His voice was very clear.

Frank grabbed his brother's arm. "Do you hear that?" he cried. "The receiver is not picking up one bit of static!"

"You're right!" Joe agreed. "It must be designed to work in the high-frequency bands."

"But how can we be receiving a broadcast direct from Madrid? That Spanish station must be transmitting by short-wave. Yet, we're hearing it loud and clear. This is amazing!"

Joe gazed at the miniature radio with great interest. "I'll bet there's a lot more to Mr Wright's invention than just being able to hear overseas stations without static," he observed. "After all, why is he so anxious to keep it a secret?"

Just then there was a loud knock on the back door and a voice from outside said, "Let me in! I'm a ham! I have a message for you!"

·3·

Warning Message

FOR a few seconds none of the Hardys spoke. They were trying to decide if the caller at the kitchen door really was a radio ham with a message. Or a member of the burglary gang?

Finally Mrs Hardy said, "We can't let the man stand out there in the rain."

Frank called, "Where's the message from?"

"Mr Hardy in San Francisco."

"Open the door," Mrs Hardy said quietly.

Joe hid the box containing the invention, then he and Frank stood on either side of the door, poised for any attack. Aunt Gertrude had armed herself with a broom. Joe turned the knob and a water-drenched figure in raincoat and hat stepped into the kitchen.

"Thanks," the man said, removing his hat. "What a night! My wife told me I was crazy to come out."

The speaker was an honest-faced man of about thirty-five. He noticed Aunt Gertrude's broom and smiled. "You can put that away," he said. "I'm harmless."

Miss Hardy looked embarrassed. "Take off your coat," she said. "I'll get you some coffee."

The man nodded. "I could use it. I got cold walking over here. My car wouldn't start."

"Did you come far?" Joe asked.

"About five blocks. I'm Larry Burton, 69 Meadow-brook Road. I've always wanted to meet the Hardy boys. This all came about in a funny way. I have a short-wave set. Tonight I picked up your father. He said he couldn't get through to you or the police on the phone—lines tied up—and you didn't answer his signal on your short-wave set."

"We weren't expecting a call," Frank answered. He did not say that he and Joe had not been at home and that their mother and Aunt Gertrude rarely paid attention to the set unless specifically asked to do so.

"By the time I phoned you, the lightning was fierce," Burton went on. "My wife's scared to death of lightning. She wouldn't let me use the phone, so I walked over."

Aunt Gertrude served the visitor coffee and cake as they all sat around the big kitchen table.

"What was the message, Mr Burton?" Joe asked.

"That you boys are in great danger. A gang is after you and will stop at nothing to get what they want."

"How dreadful!" Mrs Hardy exclaimed. "Did my husband name this—this gang?"

"No. That's all there was to the message," Burton replied. "I'm sorry to bring you bad news, but I guess that's to be expected in a detective's family. Well, I must get along." He stood up.

Frank shook the man's hand. "We sure appreciate this. Maybe some time we can return the favour."

"Forget it," Burton said. "I only hope that gang doesn't harm you fellows."

Joe helped him on with his coat and he went out. The storm had passed over.

For a few minutes the Hardys discussed the visitor and confirmed his address in the telephone directory. Joe was a bit sceptical, however. "Either he made up the whole story, or else Dad is really concerned for our safety."

Frank was inclined to think Burton had told the truth. Had he and Joe already encountered two members of the gang at the Wright home?

Aunt Gertrude spoke up. "How in the world did my brother Fenton hear this in California?"

"News travels," said Mrs Hardy. "Especially among detectives and police."

"Hmmm!" Aunt Gertrude murmured, then announced she was going to bed.

Ten minutes later Frank and Joe were asleep and did not waken until ten o'clock. At once Frank got up and opened a wooden chest of sports equipment under which he had hidden the box containing Mr Wright's invention. It was still there.

"Where do you think we should keep this?" he asked Joe as they were dressing. "Dad said not to leave the box at home."

"A tough problem, Frank. With that gang after us, we can't take the chance of carrying it round with us," Frank answered.

"Right. And they may not be after us, but after the invention," Frank answered.

While they were having breakfast, Frank came up with the idea of a unique hiding place for the invention. "Let's put it in the well under the spare tyre in the boot of our car," he said.

Joe laughed. "Now you're using that old brain of

yours. Best place you could have picked. The car's vibrations can't hurt the radio and no one would think of looking there."

Mrs Hardy asked her sons what their plans were for the day.

"Dad told us to drop into the antique aeroplane show and see if we could spot anybody who seemed overly interested," Frank replied. "He thought the person who stole Mr Wright's old plane might be planning another theft."

"Tonight," Joe continued, "we're going to Chet's party and staying until tomorrow. Okay?"

"Of course," his mother answered.

Chet Morton, an overweight, good-natured schoolmate, lived on a farm at the edge of Bayport. A group of boys and girls had been invited there to a barn dance and late supper. Frank and Joe would pick up Callie Shaw, a special friend of Frank's. His brother's date was usually Chet's sister Iola.

Mrs Hardy remarked that since the boys would be away, she would spend the night with a friend. "Your aunt plans to visit Cousin Helen in Gresham, anyhow."

During the conversation Aunt Gertrude had left the table. She returned holding the local morning newspaper. "Well, you boys are in for real trouble!" she exclaimed. "Listen to this!"

Miss Hardy read an account of the captured burglars at the Wright home and the mysterious summons to the police. The item stressed the fact that the men's assailants, when caught, should be dealt with severely.

"When caught, eh?" Joe burst into laughter. "We're going to be mighty hard to find, aren't we, Frank?"

His brother grinned, but Mrs Hardy looked worried. "Maybe you boys should explain everything to Chief Collig."

"Not without Dad's and Mr Wright's permission," Frank answered. "For the time being—"

"I haven't finished," Aunt Gertrude interrupted. "It says here that the police think this incident might be part of a gang feud." She removed her reading glasses and gazed at her nephews. "You two are now considered to be part of a gang and the rival gang is about to harm you."

"Wow!" said Joe, pulling his hair over his eyes and striking the pose of a belligerent "bad guy". "We'd better look the part!"

Since the antique aeroplane show did not open until two o'clock, the boys did various chores during the morning. They also hid Mr Wright's invention in the tyre well and bolted the spare wheel back into place.

After lunch Frank and Joe drove Aunt Gertrude to the train. From there they went directly to the Bayport Air Terminal where the antique aeroplane exhibit was housed in the spacious lobby. The first person they saw was Chet Morton.

"Hi, fellows!" he greeted them. "Say, take a look at those old planes. Aren't they beauties?"

"Sure are," Frank agreed. "I notice that most of them are biplanes. It must have been fun flying in the days of the open cockpits."

"You can say that again!" Chet declared. As he stepped back for a better view, his foot slammed down on the toe of a man standing directly behind him.

"Ow!" the stranger yelped.

The boys turned to see the man hopping about on one foot. "You stupid, overgrown kid!" he screamed.

"I'm awfully sorry," Chet said apologetically.

The tall, muscular man, who had blond hair and hard features, looked at the youth menacingly. "You idiot!" he snarled.

Frank and Joe stepped in front of Chet as he stammered, "Who—who are you calling an idiot?"

"Now just a minute!" Joe interrupted. "It was an accident. No sense getting upset about this!"

"Can I be of any help?" the boys heard someone say. They looked round to see a lanky young man walking towards them. He had rust-coloured hair and leathery skin that was deeply tanned.

"What are you butting in for?" snapped the stranger.

"This boy didn't step on you intentionally," the young man insisted. "I saw the whole thing. You were trying to listen to their conversation and got too close."

The tall stranger was about to say something, but hesitated. For a moment he glared at Chet and his companions, then stamped out of the lobby, swinging his briefcase.

Frank and Joe looked at each other. Why had the man been listening to their conversation? Did he belong to the gang they had been warned about?

Meanwhile, Chet was saying, "Thanks for your help, Mr—"

"My name is Cole Weber," the young man introduced himself. "I'm president of the Central Antique Aeroplane Club. We own the exhibit and are taking it to several airports. We're trying to encourage public interest in vintage aircraft."

"Sounds like a great club," Joe remarked.

"We think so," Weber said. "The majority of the models you see here are replicas of real aeroplanes owned and operated by our members."

"You mean that some of those old crates still fly?" Chet asked.

Weber grinned. "Well . . . we don't think of them as crates. When properly rebuilt, most antique planes are as safe and reliable as the day they were originally made. I own one myself. It's outside on the ramp. Would you like to see it?"

"Would we?" Joe exclaimed.

Mr Weber led the boys to the airport ramp. A short distance ahead stood an orange-and-white biplane. The boys peered into the two open cockpits.

"This is cool!" Joe declared.

The pilot smiled. "Compared to modern planes, mine doesn't have many instruments. But since we fly the antiques only for fun, we don't need elaborate equipment, such as that required for all-weather operations."

The boys looked closely at the diagonal pattern of wires stretching between the wings. Then they examined the plane's radial engine and the long, slender wooden propeller.

"How many passengers can you carry?" Frank asked.

"Two in the front cockpit," Weber answered. "Say! Would two of you like to go for a ride?"

The boys' eyes widened with excitement. Then Frank and Joe remembered the sleuthing they had promised to do for their father.

"Thanks just the same," Frank said, "but I'm afraid Joe and I can't go this time."

"But I'd like to," Chet spoke up. "Say, fellows, could you drive me to the farm afterwards?"

"Farm?" Weber interrupted. "Are there any level stretches of ground in the area?"

"Plenty of them. Why?"

"I'll fly you home if you'd like."

Chet tingled with excitement. "Great! Thanks."

The flier opened the baggage compartment and took out a parachute, helmet, and goggles. "Put these on and climb into the front cockpit."

"Mr Weber, do you know Mr Malcolm Wright?" Frank asked.

"Yes, indeed. He's a member of our club."

"Did you hear that his antique plane was stolen?" Joe put in.

Weber nodded. "Too bad. I understand he has some secret invention he was trying out in the plane. I hope that wasn't stolen too."

The boys caught their breath in astonishment but said nothing. They had not heard this. Weber did not seem to notice. He donned his own parachute and summoned a mechanic to twirl the propeller and start the engine. Then he climbed into the rear cockpit.

"Brakes on! Switch off!" the mechanic called.

"Brakes on! Switch off!" Weber echoed.

The mechanic pulled the propeller through several times. Then he stepped back and yelled:

"Contact!"

"Contact!" the pilot responded.

The engine caught on the first try. A staccato

popping developed into a steady roar. Chet's goggled face turned towards the Hardys. He waved wildly as Weber taxied out for take-off.

"See you at the party!" Chet shouted over the roar of the engine.

Minutes later the plane, looking like a box kite, was climbing above the Bayport field. As the Hardys turned to leave, Frank caught his brother's arm.

"There's that man Chet stepped on! He's watching us from the doorway! This time I mean to find out why." Frank started to run. "Come on, Joe!"

·4·

The Cold Trail

As soon as the man saw Frank and Joe, he turned to hurry off. In doing so, he bumped into the frame of the door and dropped his briefcase, which burst open. At a distance the boys could not read any of the printing on the letters that fell out, but one had red and blue stripes at the top.

The tall, blond man snatched up the papers and stuffed them into the briefcase. He quickly zipped it shut and began to run.

"He sure isn't on the level," Joe remarked, "or he wouldn't race off like that. We can't let him get away!"

The stranger's long legs and agility helped him cover a wide stretch in a short time. Before the Hardys could catch up to him, he reached the exit and jumped into a waiting car which zoomed off.

Frank and Joe stopped short, puzzled. Was the man afraid of them? And if so, why?

"Maybe that briefcase had something to do with his running off," Frank said.

The boys went inside the terminal building. They continued to look at the planes while keeping their eyes open for any other suspicious characters. They saw none and finally returned home.

"You must be hungry," said Mrs Hardy. "I have hot apple pie, but it's getting cold."

Joe patted her shoulder. "Shall we eat dessert first?" he teased.

Later the boys went upstairs to change for Chet's barn dance. Both put on jeans, plaid shirts, and big straw hats. They packed overnight bags, then joined their mother who was waiting to be driven to her friend's home.

Just before leaving the house, Frank heard a signal from their private short-wave set. "Dad must be calling," he said, and raced upstairs to Mr Hardy's study.

"FH home," he said into the mike. "Over."

"Frank," said his father, "how's everything?"

"Okay, Dad. How about you?"

"Fair," the detective said. "But I have a new lead to follow. You won't be able to get in touch with me for a couple of days. Did you get my message from the ham operator?"

"Yes, Dad." Frank told him all that had happened in the past twenty-four hours, including the wire-tapping.

Mr Hardy whistled. "Then the gang knew where you were going."

"Shall Joe and I tell Chief Collig we were the first burglars?" Frank asked.

"I guess you'd better," the detective agreed. "But warn him the information is confidential and don't tell him what the invention is you were after."

He now explained that he had been tipped off by Chicago police that a gang suspected of robbery there had suddenly vanished. A "squealer" had reported they were out to "get" the Hardy detectives. The boys' father did not know why, but surmised it might concern Mr Wright's invention.

"And now let me speak to your mother," Mr Hardy said.

Half an hour later Frank and Joe stopped at Chief Collig's home and made their report. The chief burst into laughter. "So you're the ones who knocked out those men. I guess they had a real scare. They haven't talked since."

By the time the boys reached the Mortons' farm with Callie Shaw, the dance was under way. A Bayport High School group was playing.

"Hi, masterminds!" Chet shouted as the Hardys strolled in. "I thought you'd never get here. Boy! Wait till I tell you about my flight!" He began to describe the adventure, supplementing his words with swooping motions of both hands.

His sister Iola joined Callie and the boys. She was a slim, dark-haired girl and very pretty. "Hi, Joe, Frank, Callie!" Then hearing her brother, she said laughingly, "Oh no! Is Chet talking about his flight again? He hasn't stopped since he landed."

"You just don't know anything about real flying," her brother said, "until you've been in one of those old biplanes."

"Our turn's next," Joe reminded him.

The following hours passed quickly When it was time for supper, Joe and Iola decided to eat outside. They filled their paper plates with sandwiches, chocolate cake and cups of lemonade, and went to sit on the steps of the Mortons' front veranda.

As they ate, Iola glanced towards the driveway in which many of the guests had parked their cars. The Hardys' convertible was near the end of the long queue.

Suddenly Iola touched Joe's arm. "What's the matter?" he asked.

"I saw someone lurking behind your car," Iola replied. "Yes, There he is."

Joe peered into the darkness. He saw a man, his hat pulled low, pop up from behind the car, then duck down again. At once the young detective sprang to his feet and ran towards the mysterious figure. The fellow might be after the secret radio!

"Who are you?" he shouted, seeing the boot lid rise and the light go on. "What are you doing?"

The intruder ran from behind the car and disappeared into the darkness. Joe dashed after him.

"Keep your distance or you'll get hurt!" the man shouted. But Joe went on.

Iola screamed for help. Frank, Chet, and their classmates, Biff Hooper and Jerry Gilroy, raced from the barn.

"What's wrong?" Frank asked.

"We saw a man lurking behind your car," Iola answered in a trembling voice. "Joe ran after him through the woods but was warned away."

At once Frank and his companions rushed in that direction. The boys had not gone far when they heard a muffled cry for help, followed by the roar of a car speeding off.

Coming to a halt, Frank signalled to his friends for silence. The sounds of the car faded away. Everything was still, except the big grandfather clock in the hall of the Morton home. It began to strike. Midnight! Frank thought of what had happened just twenty-four hours earlier.

"Joe!" he shouted. "Joe! Where are you?"

His call went unanswered. The young detective stood frozen in his tracks. Had his brother become the victim of the gang?

By this time everyone at the party had raced outside to learn what had happened. They joined in a frantic search but without success.

"I'm afraid he was kidnapped," Frank said grimly.

"In the car we heard roar off?" Biff Hooper asked.

"Yes."

Jerry Gilroy chimed in, "But by whom? And for what reason?"

"I don't know," Frank said. He turned and rushed back to the convertible. Seeing the boot open, he immediately looked in the tyre well. The secret radio was still there.

"Joe must have blocked an attempted theft and been taken away so that he couldn't identify the man," Frank thought.

He slammed the boot shut, asked his friends to guard the car, and ran to the house. He scooped up the telephone and dialled the home number of Chief Collig.

"What!" the officer exclaimed when Frank told him about Joe's probable kidnapping. "I'll call the FBI and also get some of my own men out there right away! And I'll come myself."

He and three officers arrived shortly and were given a briefing. The place was carefully examined, but the searchlights picked up little.

There was such a profusion of tyre tracks on the main road that those of the mystery car could not be detected. Iola, the only one except Joe who had seen the suspect, could give little information other than that he was tall, heavy set, and wore gloves.

"Then we won't find any fingerprints on your car," the chief said to Frank.

Frank nodded. "He could be the man who ran from Joe and me at the airport." Frank told the police about him and gave a fuller description.

"We'll be on the lookout for him, as well as for Joe," Collig said. "There's nothing more we can do here, but I'll leave two of my men."

Solemnly the group left the barn dance and each guest expressed a hope for Joe's speedy return. The Mortons tried to comfort Frank and discussed whether or not they should call Mrs Hardy and tell her the disturbing news.

"I don't see that anything can be gained by that," Chet's mother said. "Let's wait."

She insisted Frank try to get some sleep, but he lay wide awake, hoping the phone would ring with good news from Collig. But none came. Chet, in the same room, was restless.

Finally at five o'clock he said, "Where do we go from here?"

"I'm not sure." Frank sighed. "We've absolutely no clue. In fact, we don't even have a description of the car we heard drive off last night."

"Joe could be miles from here by now," his chum remarked.

Frank thought for a moment. "Let's drive down the

road and make some inquiries at the farmhouses along the way. There's a slim chance someone may have spotted the kidnap car."

The boys left the house quietly and jumped into the Hardys' convertible. They waved to the patrolling police guards. Frank drove along the narrow, tree-lined road. As they feared, all their inquiries were fruitless. Most of the farmers they questioned had retired long before midnight, and had neither seen nor heard anything.

"Guess we may as well go home," Chet suggested.

But Frank was not ready to give up. "Let's drive on a little farther," he said.

About six-thirty, the boys spotted a farmer cutting weeds by the roadside and stopped to question him. He rubbed his chin dubiously while listening to their story.

"Quite a few cars go past my place every night," he said. "But now you come to mention it, there was an automobile came whizzin' along and stopped here right after midnight. It woke me up, what with two men in it shoutin' at each other."

"Did you see the car?" Frank asked.

"No. I didn't get up. Course my home is right beside the road, and I couldn't help but hear some o' what the men were sayin'. The car come along at a mighty lively clip, but when it got in front of the house, the driver slammed on the brakes and stopped.

"There was an argument. I heard him tellin' somebody they must have gone past the crossroads in the dark. The other man started jawin' at him and they had quite a row. Finally they turned the car round and went back."

"To the crossroads?" said Chet.

"Yes. That's about two miles back."

"I remember. One road goes to Gresham, the other heads up through the market gardens."

Frank and Chet returned to the crossroads. But which way should they go? Right to the market gardens, left to Gresham?

"The kidnappers might have hidden Joe on one of the market gardens," Chet suggested.

"Yes, except that all those farms are close together and everybody knows everybody else's business," said Frank. "I'd rather tackle the road to Gresham. If we don't find Joe, we can come back and try the other road." He took the turn to the left.

As they sped along, the boys spotted the wreckage of a black car in a roadside ditch. Afraid that this was the kidnap car, Frank pulled up.

"Some accident!" Chet observed.

The licence plates had already been removed from the badly smashed-up car.

"If anybody was hurt," Frank said, "they'll know it in Gresham. We'll ask the police there."

Suddenly a black saloon swung out of a lane some distance ahead and roared off towards the town. Frank stared fixedly at the back seat.

"Look!" he exclaimed, gripping Chet's arm. "Do you see what I see?"

"What?"

"A hand. Isn't that someone signalling?"

Chet gazed ahead and saw a hand wave frantically for a moment at the rear window, then suddenly withdraw.

"You're right!" Chet snapped. "Joe!"

Frank started the convertible and sped off in pursuit.

The other car had a good lead and was increasing speed. It was almost obscured by a cloud of dust, but Frank memorized the out-of-state licence number.

"We're gaining on them!" Chet declared.

Frank nodded. Inch by inch the intervening distance lessened. Trees, farms, and hedges flashed by. At times the boys could hardly see the saloon through the swirling clouds of dust.

Suddenly the steady hum of the convertible's engine changed its rhythm. The motor spluttered.

Chet groaned. "Now what?" he muttered as the car slowed down.

The boys' hearts sank when the engine stopped completely. They looked dismally at the other car as it disappeared round a distant bend in the road.

· 5 ·

The Hunt

FRANTICALLY Frank flung open the hood and examined the engine. In a few minutes he discovered the trouble.

"Fuel pump," he announced.

"Oh—oh!" Chet sighed. "And we're miles from a service garage."

"We're not stranded," Frank assured him. "I suspected the pump was going so I put a spare in the boot. But it's going to take fifteen or twenty minutes to change the pump, and—"

"And by that time the kidnap car will be far away," Chet finished.

"I'd better notify Bayport Police Headquarters." Frank turned on the car's two-way radio to the proper frequency and gave the licence number of the suspect's car.

"We'll get busy on it right away," came the answer. "Incidentally, FBI men have been here and out to the Morton farm. I'll contact them. There's no news so far."

Frank replaced the mike. He and Chet worked feverishly to install the new fuel pump and soon had the engine running.

"No chance of our catching up with the saloon now,"

Chet remarked as the boys once again got under way. "It has nearly half an hour's head start."

"I'll bet that the kidnappers won't stop at Gresham, now that they've learned we're after them."

Ten minutes later Frank stopped the car. He backed into a side road, pulled out again, then turned to retrace his route. "I want to go up that lane the kidnap car came out of and see what we can find."

Reaching it, Frank turned in. The ground was stony and full of holes. Progress was slow.

Half a mile farther on, an old inn, apparently closed, came into view. It was a long, low, white building with a wide veranda. The boys got out of the car and Frank knocked several times, hoping someone might be inside. There was no response.

"Nobody's home," Chet mumbled.

Just then the sound of heavy footsteps could be heard. The door sprang open and a surly-faced man confronted them.

"What is it?" he growled.

"Sorry to bother you, sir," Frank said, "but have you seen a black four-door saloon within the past hour?"

"You've got a nerve waking me up to ask such a stupid question!" the man snapped. "I don't know anything about a saloon!"

"Have you had any visitors recently?" Frank persisted. "There's a wrecked car lying in a ditch close to the spot where your lane leads in from the road. Did anyone come here for help?"

The man looked at the boys suspiciously. "Get out of here before I kick you off the porch!"

"Have it your way!" Frank retorted. "I'm certain

"Get out of here before I kick you off the porch!"
the man growled.

there were kidnappers in that saloon I asked you about. If you know anything, you'd better tell me, or be held as an accessory!"

"Kidnappers?" the man cried out. "Okay! So there were some guys walked in here late last night."

"How many were there?" Frank demanded.

"Three. One said they'd had an accident, and asked if they could stay at my place for a while. They paid me real good, so I let 'em come in."

"Please describe these men."

"One was tall, one short," the proprietor replied nervously. "The big guy said they're brothers named Wagner. They were carrying the third guy—he was wrapped in a blanket 'cause he got knocked out. I couldn't see his face. The big guy made a telephone call to Gresham. A car picked 'em up about an hour and a half ago. I can't tell you any more!"

He stepped back inside the house and slammed the door in the boys' faces.

"Sociable guy," Chet commented as the boys drove off. "He did give us one lead," Frank said. "The wreck was theirs and the pickup car came from the direction of Gresham. Chet, I'm afraid Joe was hurt. We're going to Gresham. I'll call Collig and tell him what we've just heard." He tuned in Bayport headquarters and left the message.

On reaching Gresham, Frank cruised up and down the side streets flanking the main boulevard, hoping to spot the saloon but had no luck. He then headed for the local police headquarters. "Dad introduced me to Police Chief Stanton when we were passing through this town several months ago," he said.

The boys entered the neat, red-brick building and Frank introduced himself and Chet to the desk sergeant on duty. They were ushered into the office of the chief.

"Frank Hardy, how are you?" Stanton said, extending his hand in greeting. "Sit down."

"Has Chief Collig in Bayport been in touch with you?" Frank asked.

"Yes. So far we have no word on the saloon or the men travelling in it, one of them injured. You're sure your brother was kidnapped?"

"Without a doubt!"

"Hmm!" Stanton muttered. "The saloon's probably miles away by now with a different licence plate. But our men will keep on the lookout."

Realizing they could do no more here, Frank and Chet decided to return to Bayport.

"What's our next move?" Chet asked.

"Whoever kidnapped Joe might ask for ransom, Chet. I'd better stick close to the phone at home in case someone tries to establish contact."

Then Frank's heart sank as he thought of having to tell his mother and father and aunt that Joe was missing! When he pulled into the Hardy garage some time later, Frank shut off the ignition and sat quiet for several seconds. Then he took a deep breath and climbed out of the car.

He had no sooner entered the house when Mrs Hardy rushed to meet him. "What happened to Joe?" she cried.

Frank was startled by her question. Before answering, he hugged his mother and led her into the living room.

"I'd just got home, and decided to telephone the

Morton farm. I spoke to Iola," Mrs Hardy explained. "She seemed terribly upset and started to tell me something about Joe, then stopped. She said you were on your way here and would explain."

Frank related the whole story of Joe's disappearance. Mrs Hardy was stunned by the news and tears filled her eyes.

"I would have told you sooner," Frank said, "but I was hoping to find Joe before this."

Although Mrs Hardy worried about the dangers involved in her family's sleuthing activities, she rarely displayed her concern openly. But now she could not hide her anxiety. She began to tremble.

"We must do something!" she pleaded. "Have you notified the police?"

"Yes," Frank answered. "And the FBI."

"Your father! He should be told about this at once!"

"But we can't reach him," Frank reminded her.

The hours dragged on into early evening. Mrs Hardy continually walked the floor, saying over and over, "This is dreadful, dreadful!"

Frank paced around nervously, mulling over in his mind the events that had taken place during the past two days. The telephone rang. Was it the kidnapper calling? Frank rushed to answer the call.

"Frank, this is Chief Collig!"

"Yes, Chief! Any news?"

"Not much. The police managed to detect the scratched-off serial number on the engine block of the car lying in the ditch. It was traced through the State Bureau of Motor Vehicles. The car was stolen yesterday evening from a man in Lewiston. No one saw the thief."

"Well, we're right back where we started," Frank said.

After a light late supper, Frank settled himself into a wing chair within reach of the telephone. The hours ticked by with no word from Joe or his abductors. Finally, through sheer exhaustion, Frank dozed off.

When he awoke, the sun was already sending bright, warm rays into the room. Frank got up and began to pace back and forth. He and his mother ate a sketchy breakfast. They grew more uneasy when the morning passed without any news of Joe.

Shortly after noon a taxi stopped in front of the Hardy home. A tall, angular woman, carrying a small suitcase, got out of the cab and hurried towards the house.

"It's Aunt Gertrude," Frank announced to his mother.

"I'm glad to be home!" Miss Hardy exclaimed as she entered the house like a rush of wind.

She glanced at Mrs Hardy and immediately sensed that something was troubling her. "Laura! You look exhausted. Haven't you been getting enough sleep? What's wrong?"

"We have something to tell you," Frank declared. "You'd better sit down."

He broke the news about Joe's disappearance as gently as he could. His story, however, sent Aunt Gertrude springing from her chair.

"That's terrible! Poor Joe! Call the police!" she cried. "Call the FBI! Do something!"

"Try to be calm," Frank pleaded. "The police and the FBI have already been notified."

"I felt it in my bones!" Aunt Gertrude exclaimed. "Something like this was bound to happen."

"Now, Gertrude, please," Mrs Hardy interrupted.

Aunt Gertrude continued to rattle on. "You can't be too careful these days. The world is full of rude and nasty people. Now you take this morning, for example, when I was walking on the platform at Gresham. Suddenly this big, fair-haired man stepped right in front of me, carrying a bulging briefcase. Part of its zipper was torn and some of the papers inside were sticking through.

"Well, this clumsy ox gave me a hard bang on my arm with that dirty, beat-up briefcase. I was about to give him a piece of my mind, when he deliberately pushed me aside!"

Her words had seized Frank's attention. The man sounded like the one that Chet had stepped on in the airport terminal and Frank and Joe had chased later. He might be one of the kidnappers! The suspects' car had gone towards Gresham!

"Then came the crowning insult," she went on. "He called me—he called me—an old whaler! Can you imagine? I never fished for a whale in my life! Next, this big, fair-haired lummox walked over to two other men and handed them the briefcase," Aunt Gertrude continued. "I was so furious, I decided to demand an apology. I went up to the big man and tapped him on the shoulder. He must know me because just then he said 'Hardy'. Well, he turned and glared at me, then hurried off with his friends. The nerve, indeed!"

Frank had already jumped to his feet. He was obviously excited. "Did you see what was written on the papers in the briefcase?"

"I wasn't close enough to read them. But one had red and blue stripes on it."

"He's one of the men we suspect!" Frank cried out. "Aunty, did you hear any more of the men's conversation? Anything at all?"

"No, not really," she answered, somewhat puzzled by her nephew's questioning. "I only caught a word or two. The fair-haired man said something about caves. Yes, that's it—caves! I remember because it struck me at the time that with his bad manners, he should be living in one."

Frank darted to the telephone and called Chet. "I'm sure I've latched on to an important lead," he told his chum. "I'll need your help."

"I'm ready to go any time you say."

"Okay! I'll be right over!"

· 6 ·

Fogged In

FRANK leaped into the convertible and headed for the Morton farm. He began piecing together the details of Aunt Gertrude's story about the fair-haired man at Gresham. He had said, "Hardy!"

"I'm sure he didn't mean Aunt Gertrude. He could have meant Dad or Joe!"

Then the man had made a reference to caves! There were many to be found in the cliffs which formed the north shore of Barmet Bay. Was Joe being held in one of them? Frank smiled, recalling his aunt's indignation at being called an "old whaler" by the big fair-haired man.

"He might not have been referring to whales at all," Frank thought. "There's a small, flat-hulled motorboat known as a motor whaler. Maybe that's what he had in mind."

Frank told himself that using such a term would be unusual for any person unless he was familiar with boats. The young sleuth was certain that he had a real lead at last!

As Frank drew up before the Morton house, Chet came down the steps at a run. "What's up?" he asked eagerly.

Frank repeated Aunt Gertrude's story of the man mentioning the name Hardy and making the mysterious reference to whaler and caves.

Chet whistled, then suddenly his eyes widened. "You mean Joe might be a prisoner in a shore cave?"

"Exactly!" Frank answered. "And I'll search every one of them if I have to!"

"I'm with you! How about the other fellows? Let's get Biff and Jerry to come along. They'd be mad as hornets if they weren't in on the search."

"Okay!" Frank replied. "We'll use the *Sleuth*." This was the Hardys' sleek motorboat.

"Let's go!" Chet said briskly. Then the ever-present problem of food occurred to him. "If you'll wait a few minutes I'll ask Mom to fix up a lunch for us. We may get hungry. At least you *may*, but I'm sure I will."

Both boys dashed into the house. While Mrs Morton was making up a package of sandwiches and cake, Frank reached Jerry and Biff by telephone and gave them an inkling of what was afoot. They were eager to help and promised to be at the Hardy boathouse within twenty minutes.

In a short time Chet was ready and scrambled into the convertible beside Frank. At the boathouse Jerry and Biff were waiting for them. Biff was a tall, lanky blond whose perpetual good humour was indicated by the slight tilt to the outer corners of his lips. Jerry, medium height and dark, was wiry and more serious. Both boys were agog with curiosity.

"What's the clue?" Jerry asked, and Frank gave the details as he unlocked the door of the boathouse.

The boys quickly unmoored the *Sleuth* and jumped

aboard. The engine spluttered spasmodically a few times, then burst into a roar. Frank opened the throttle and the craft shot into the bay, gradually increasing speed.

"If we don't find Joe, then what?" Jerry asked.

Frank answered promptly, "Go down the coast tomorrow. There are a few caves along the beach. You fellows game?"

"You bet," they chorused.

There were clouds in the sky and far off towards the open water at the distant end of the bay was a hint of fog. Frank eyed the mist doubtfully. It would take some time to make a close search of the caves on the north shore, and if fog came up, a hunt would be difficult. Chet, thinking the same thing, mentioned it aloud.

"We'll just have to hope for the best," Biff spoke up.

As they zipped along, the boys talked over Miss Hardy's encounter with the fair-haired man.

"He may be tall," said Biff, "but he sure sounds short on brains!"

"He'll need all the brains he has if we get on his trail," Chet affirmed.

"But why would he be mixed up in Joe's disappearance?" said Biff. "Surely he wouldn't kidnap Joe just because Chet stepped on him."

"There's something deeper behind it," Frank said, thinking of the secret radio, "but I'm not at liberty to tell you fellows. Sorry."

The *Sleuth* sped on towards the north shore and gradually drew closer to the high cliffs that rose sheer from the waters of the bay. The fog was coming up the bay now in a high, menacing grey wall.

Chet grimaced. "We're not going to make it. That fog will be on us before we get within a quarter of a mile of the caves."

"I'm afraid so," Frank said. "But I hate to give up now that we've come this far."

"I've had a few experiences in fog out on this bay," Biff Hooper remarked, "and I don't want to repeat 'em if it can be helped. You never know when some other boat is going to come along and run you down. You can't see it until the boat's right on top of you. Let one of those big ships wallop you and you're done for!"

"A horn isn't much good," said Jerry, "because the fog seems to make the sound come from a different direction than the true one."

The fog swirled down on the boys, hiding the shore from view. It enveloped them so completely that they could scarcely see more than a few yards ahead. Frank had already turned on his yellow fog light and suddenly they saw a small tug a short distance up the bay. The craft was heading towards the city, but now it vanished. Frank reduced speed and pressed the horn. No sound!

"This," said Jerry, "is bad. If it weren't for Joe, I'd say go home. I wonder how long the pea soup will last."

No one ventured a guess. Frank said tensely, "Watch for that tug, fellows. My horn won't blow."

As the *Sleuth* groped blindly through the clammy mist, Frank thought he heard the faint throb of the tug's engines. His light did not pick up the craft and it was impossible to estimate its distance or direction.

Then came the blast of the tug's whistle, low and mournful through the heavy fog. It seemed to be far to the right, and Frank hoped to avoid it by going straight ahead.

When the whistle sounded again, it was louder and seemed to come from a point just to their left. It was drawing closer!

"That old tug must have travelled about two miles clean across the bay in half a minute," Chet remarked. "Frank, I—look out!"

As he spoke, the whistle sounded again. This time Biff straightened up in alarm. The tug seemed to be directly ahead.

"How do you figure its position, Frank?"

"I think the tug is mighty close. It's hard to tell where the sound's coming from. We'll just have to go easy and hope we see it first."

Biff could hardly make out the stern of the *Sleuth*. "This is worse than a blackout," he commented.

Once more the whistle blew, this time so terrifyingly loud that the tug seemed to be only a few yards away. The boys could hear its engines. Still their light revealed nothing.

"Up in front, Chet!" snapped Frank. "If you see it, sing out!"

Chet scrambled on to the bow and peered into the grey gloom ahead. Suddenly, he gave a yell of terror.

"It's bearing right down on us!"

Even as he shouted, a heavy dark shadow loomed out of the fog. The *Sleuth* was about to be rammed!

The tug was sweeping down on the boys. It was only a few yards away! The boys could see a man on deck, waving his arms wildly. The whistle shrieked.

No time to lose! The engine of the *Sleuth* broke into a

sudden clamour as Frank opened the throttle wide. At the same instant he swung the wheel hard to port. The motorboat swerved and shot directly across the bow of the larger boat.

For a breathless second it seemed that nothing could save the boys. They waited for the jarring impact that seemed only seconds away!

But the *Sleuth* had speed, and Frank handled his craft masterfully. His boat shot clear!

The tug went roaring astern. It had missed the *Sleuth* with less than a yard to spare! The Hardys' boat was caught in the heavy swell and pitched to and fro, but rode it out.

Chet Morton broke the silence. "Wow, that was a close call!"

Jerry Gilroy, who had been thrown off balance when the *Sleuth* altered its course so suddenly, scrambled to his feet, blinking. "I'll say! Were we hit?"

"We're still here." Biff grinned. Nevertheless, he had been badly frightened. "That's the last time I'll ever come out on the bay when there's a fog brewing," he announced solemnly. "That was too narrow a squeak!"

Chet, now that the peril had passed, leaned down from the bow. He shook hands with the other three boys, then gravely clasped his own.

"What's that for?" Jerry asked.

"Congratulating you—and myself on still being alive." The others smiled weakly.

Frank steered the *Sleuth* back to its previous course. Again the boat crept towards the north shore, invisible beyond the wall of mist. Frank did not dare venture closer for fear of piling his craft on to the rocks at the foot of the cliffs. He cruised aimlessly back and forth, but within half an hour the fog began to lift. It thinned out, writhing and twisting like plumes of smoke.

"The cliffs!" Chet cried in relief as the boys caught sight of the land rising sharply just ahead. They were less than two hundred yards off shore and already far down the bay, abreast of the caves.

"We can make our search after all," Frank said.

He brought the *Sleuth* as near the base of the cliffs as he dared, skilfully avoiding the menacing black rocks that thrust above the water.

Jerry, who had scrambled out on the bow, gestured towards an outcropping of rocks about a hundred yards away.

"Here's our first cave," he announced.

"I remember it," said Frank. "Joe and I went into that one when we were on a car-theft case. It looks like a cave, but is only a few feet deep. No use looking here."

The searchers passed several shallow openings, but at last Chet gave a jubilant shout. "Here're the deeper ones!"

They had rounded a little promontory and the boys saw a ragged row of gaping holes in the face of the rock. Most were just a few feet above the waterline.

Chet said, "I know them. Some are small but others are big enough for an elephant to walk through sideways."

Frank brought the *Sleuth* in still closer to the base of the two-hundred-foot-high cliffs.

"Great place to hide someone," Biff commented. "I bet there are hundreds of those caverns."

"We have our work cut out for us," Frank agreed.

Some distance on, he spotted the first of the larger holes in the rock. The cave was six feet wide and high above the water. Frank ran the boat in close enough so that by scrambling over its bow one could land on the tumbled heaps of rocks and boulders just beneath the opening.

"Let's take a look," he said eagerly. "Jerry, will you hold the boat here?"

"Sure. Go ahead."

Within a few minutes the others were climbing up the boulders towards the cave mouth. Presently they vanished into the dark interior.

·7·

The Escape

JERRY held the nose of the *Sleuth* inshore and manœuvred so that the propeller remained in deep water. He waited impatiently for news of Joe.

It did not take the others long to find that the big cave they had entered was unoccupied. They reappeared a few minutes later.

"Did you find him?" Jerry called.

"No luck," Biff reported.

Chet was discouraged and said so. "We're working on the slimmest of clues," he said. "The fair-haired man and his friends might not have meant the Shore Road caves. Don't forget, there are hundreds of subterranean caverns between Gresham and Bayport."

"But the caves here are the best known," Frank remarked. "Let's look some more. I'll cruise along the shore and pick out the more likely caves to hide a prisoner."

The motorboat edged its way along the face of the cliff. Whenever the boys noticed one of the larger openings that could be reached easily from the shore, Frank ran the boat in among the rocks. Then, while one boy stayed in the *Sleuth*, the others would scramble up to investigate the cave.

The hours dragged by. Finally, they navigated to a place where the cliff sloped and began to give way to sandy hills and wooded inclines.

Biff gave a sigh. "Guess we'll have to give up. There's only one small opening left to investigate."

"But why would kidnappers go up to that cave when there are so many that are easier to reach?" Chet protested. "They'd have to climb fifty feet up to the mouth."

"It isn't as steep as it looks," Frank remarked thoughtfully. "And I can see a winding trail up the slope."

"I'm game," Jerry said.

"Me too," Biff added.

Frank brought the *Sleuth* in towards the rocks. The boys craned their necks to look up at the tiny opening in the face of the cliff above.

"I guess you're right, Chet," Jerry admitted. "Joe's kidnappers wouldn't climb all the way up there, with so many better caves to pick from."

Chet gave a loud groan. "I've lost about three pounds already, climbing these cliffs."

Despite the worry over Joe, Biff could not refrain from saying, "Then, Chet, you'd better tackle about fifty more caves."

Frank, meanwhile, had seen something that had gone unnoticed by his friends. A piece of newspaper was lodged among the stones under the cave's mouth. The scrap of paper might be significant! The fact that it was within a few feet of the cave was suspicious and warranted investigation.

This time Chet volunteered to stand watch and

manœuvred the boat round so that the others could reach the shore from the bow. Frank went first. Biff and Jerry followed.

They climbed the slope, following the trail Frank had spotted. But the incline was so steep and winding that they could make only slow progress in a diagonal direction. The path ended abruptly at a ledge some fifteen feet below the cave. From there they had to climb directly upwards over the rocks.

When Frank reached the piece of newspaper, he picked it up. The sheet was wet and soggy from the fog, but he recognized it as a copy of the *Gresham Times*, dated the previous day.

His hopes rose with this discovery. Gresham! For the third time since Joe's disappearance the name of that town had come into the mystery! Excited, Frank thrust the paper into his pocket and scrambled up towards the entrance of the cave.

"What did you find?" Jerry demanded, panting.

"Newspaper. It looks like a clue."

Frank reached the cave mouth and stepped inside. The interior was larger than he had thought. Though the entrance was small, the cave widened and seemed to be very deep.

The young detective took a flashlight from his pocket and clicked it. He played the beam on the rugged, rocky walls, the fairly level floor, and finally focused on a wooden box like those used for shipping food.

"Someone's been here!" he shouted eagerly as the others entered the cave. "Look at that box! Fresh bread crusts around it!"

"Don't see anyone now," Jerry observed. "Listen!"

The boys heard a peculiar sound, which seemed to come from the back of the cave. The sound was repeated. They listened, staring at one another in surprise.

"Someone's groaning!" Frank exclaimed.

Biff pointed a trembling finger toward a large section of rock about twenty feet away. "From there."

Again they heard groaning.

"Somebody's behind there!" Frank declared.

He ran towards the mass of rocks and directed the light into the shadows beyond. Frank gasped as its beam fell upon a figure lying bound and gagged on a crude pallet of sacking.

"Joe!" Frank shouted. He sprang forward and removed the gag.

His brother answered feebly, "Frank!"

Biff and Jerry gave a joint yell of delight. They scrambled in behind the wall of rocks and bent over their friend.

Joe looked white and ill. He could scarcely talk to them. His feet were bound together with rope and his hands were tied behind his back.

"To think that we weren't going to search this cave at all!" Biff exclaimed. "And wait until Chet learns we've found you. He's down there guarding the *Sleuth*."

Frank had already opened his pocketknife and was hacking at the ropes that bound his brother's ankles. Jerry was working at the other knots.

"I'm hungry," said Joe, when all the ropes had been loosened and he was able to sit up. "I haven't had anything to eat since yesterday noon."

The boys helped him to his feet. "They drugged me," Joe went on shakily, "and I can still feel the effects. But tell me, how did you find me?"

"Aunt Gertrude gets the credit." Frank quickly told of her encounter with the fair-haired man at Gresham, and his reference to "Hardy" and "caves".

"But Frank put two and two together," Biff spoke up, and mentioned the newspaper clue.

"It was lucky for me you saw the paper," Joe declared. "One of the kidnappers had some food wrapped in a newspaper yesterday. He must have dropped one of the sheets."

"Was the big, fair-haired man really mixed up in it?" Frank asked.

Joe nodded. "He was in it, all right. But there were others. They were after that secret in our car. It's a long story. Let me tell you about it later."

The boys refrained from asking more questions.

"Do you feel strong enough to come with us now?" Frank asked.

Joe, with a flash of spirit, started to walk. He wavered for a moment and would have fallen if Frank had not caught him.

"If you can't make it, we'll carry you," Jerry offered.

Joe shook his head and sat down weakly. "My legs are so numb from being tied up, I don't seem to have any strength in them. I'd better wait a few minutes."

At that moment they heard a loud noise. It was a clattering, rolling sound, as if a rock had been dislodged and gone tumbling down the steep incline.

"What was that?" Biff whispered.

Joe got to his feet. "My captors are coming back! Quick! We'll have to clear out!"

"Can they get in here through the rear of the cave?" Frank wanted to know.

"Yes, a passage leads down from the top of the cliff."

Frank and Jerry each slipped an arm round Joe's shoulders and helped him towards the mouth of the cave. Biff ran on ahead.

When Chet saw Joe, he gave a war whoop of joy. The others motioned frantically for silence, but their jubilant chum did not understand their urgent signals. He proceeded to put on a noisy celebration. He yelled, waved his arms, and then, to their horror, began whistling shrilly.

The men coming down the passage into the cave would certainly hear the commotion and hurry to investigate. The boys must flee quickly!

Frank and Jerry scrambled down the slope with Joe. They reached the first ledge in safety, with Biff slipping and sliding along the path ahead of them. As they commenced the second half of the descent the boys heard a yell behind them.

Frank looked back. A man was standing at the mouth of the cave. He glared at the boys a moment, then turned and shouted to someone behind him. Two other men quickly joined him.

"Go on!" Joe cried. "I'm holding you up! If they catch us, we'll all be in trouble."

"Leave you, my eye!" Jerry growled.

By this time Biff had nearly reached the boat. He called out to Chet, who apparently had not seen the men in the mouth of the cave. At Biff's warning, Chet stopped his noise. Frank and Jerry clung to Joe on the narrow path, with loose rocks sliding treacherously beneath their feet.

Frank glanced back again. One of the men had drawn a revolver from his pocket and was pointing it at them. Another had stooped and was snatching up stones.

The revolver barked. A bullet whistled overhead. Frank and Jerry ducked and almost lost hold of Joe. A heavy stone hurtled past them and splashed into the water beside the boat.

A hail of stones followed. The man with the revolver fired again and again and several bullets came dangerously close to their mark.

Chet had revved up the engine, ready to take off as soon as his passengers climbed aboard.

"Hurry!" Biff yelled. "Only a few yards more!"

Frank and Jerry scrambled to the bottom of the incline with Joe. One of the three men was stumbling down the path in pursuit.

Jerry leaped on to the bow. With Frank on the shore and Jerry helping from the boat, Joe was hauled aboard. Frank was about to jump on to the bow when he felt a heavy, sharp blow on his left leg. He lost his balance and fell partly into the water. When he tried to rise, his leg doubled beneath him. One of the rocks hurled by the men had found its mark!

Shots sounded again. A splinter flew from the bow of the boat.

"Hurry, Frank!" Chet urged.

"Give me a hand," Frank said grimly.

Biff scrambled over the side, seized Frank, and laid

him on deck. Frank's leg throbbed and he could scarcely keep from crying out.

The man on the path was only a few yards away now! He showered the air with rocks!

·8·

An Astounding Report

SMACK! A large rock hit the water with a resounding crash only inches from the *Sleuth*. A deluge of spray drenched the boys.

Chet, at the helm, could hardly see. Wiping the water from his eyes, he revved the motor and took off. The *Sleuth* made sternway from shore.

"Gadzooks!" cried Jerry, mopping his face and looking towards the kidnappers. "They've gone!"

"They sure disappeared in a hurry," said Jerry. "I wish we could have captured them. Frank, how's your leg?"

"Oh, it'll be all right, but it hurts." He gave a wan smile. "Never mind that, though. The main thing is that we found Joe."

"Yes, thank goodness," his brother said weakly.

Chet had taken the *Sleuth* into deep water and was now speeding towards Bayport. Jerry and Biff were busy trying to make Frank and Joe comfortable on one of the long seats.

"To think I missed finding Joe!" Chet said in disgust. "I climbed those cliffs every other time and searched. When Joe was found, where was I? Sitting in the boat!"

"Good thing you were," Jerry retorted. "It's lucky

for us someone was here to have the *Sleuth* ready for a fast getaway."

"Why did it have to be me?" Chet complained. "Some fellows have all the luck. Joe, tell me about your capture. Who were those men who shot at you and heaved all those rocks? When did they take you to the cave?"

"Better let Joe rest awhile," Frank advised.

"I think we ought to go back and clean up on that gang!" Jerry put in.

"I'd like to learn more about them myself," Frank said, "but I think we'd better leave it to the police. Those kidnappers are a tough outfit, and we have Joe to look after. He's in bad shape. We should get him home."

"He looks hungry," Chet observed sympathetically, as Frank tuned in their radio and called police headquarters to report the rescue.

Joe opened his eyes. "You bet I'm hungry."

Chet grabbed the package of sandwiches he had brought with him and handed them to his chum. "I knew these would come in handy," he said. "Dig in."

"Hold it!" Frank warned. "No solid food until the doctor says it's all right."

"Then how about the milk in this Thermos?"

"Okay."

Joe drank the milk slowly and gratefully while Jerry satisfied Chet's curiosity about their experience in the cave rescue.

Chet whistled. "That was a close squeak."

When the Hardys reached home, their mother was overwhelmed with relief at seeing Joe safe.

Aunt Gertrude hugged her nephew and said, "Well, this time you deserve sympathy. At least you didn't do something harum-scarum and propel yourself right into a mess of trouble."

Dr Bates, the family physician, was summoned to examine the young detectives. "No internal damage," he declared. "Just exhaustion. Joe'll be fit in just a day or two. Frank has a deep bruise which will be sore for a while."

Joe was given a steaming bowl of hot soup, then put to bed. He immediately fell asleep.

Frank related the story of the rescue and gave Aunt Gertrude credit for the clue. She smiled and blushed but said nothing.

It was not until late that evening, after he had been refreshed by a long, sound sleep, that Joe was able to tell the others what had happened to him. He still looked pale, but good food and rest were beginning to do their work and a trace of colour had returned to his cheeks.

"As you know," he said, "at Chet's party I chased into the woods after that man who was looking in our car boot. As I got near, someone reached out and grabbed me. I couldn't see his face."

Joe said a gag had been jammed into his mouth and a hand clapped over it. Then he was dragged to a car.

"Mercy!" exclaimed Aunt Gertrude.

"But why did he kidnap you if he was only after the secret radio?" Frank asked.

"There's another reason," Joe replied. "I'll come to that. When we got to his car I tried to fight him, but he's as strong as an ox and managed to tie me up and put me in the back seat.

"Then he drove away. We went down the road for some distance and stopped. Two men came out of the bushes and walked over to us. One said, 'Is that you, Gross?' and my captor growled at them, 'No names.' When they saw me in the car, the men wanted to know who I was. It seems they didn't know Gross was going to kidnap me."

Joe said there had been a row about it. The other two men had wanted Gross to bring him back, but he was stubborn. "This kid knows too much," Gross had said. "He saw the rocks. Besides, his father is a detective."

"The other men called him a fool and said he should have left me alone and let the other thing go.

"One of them told Gross they didn't want the authorities after them for kidnapping. Then they realized it was too late to let me go, because there would be trouble when I got back to Bayport and told my story."

Joe said that the two men got into the car and they all rode for about two miles. Then one of the men climbed out and headed across a field towards the bay.

"We went on, but we hadn't gone far when Gross lost control of the wheel and we crashed into a ditch. The car was wrecked but no one was hurt. Gross and the other man seemed worried because they were afraid somebody would come along and find them. They took off the licence plates.

"Gross knew there was an old inn nearby. They agreed to go to it and telephone a friend of theirs to bring a saloon. They took a blanket out of the car. We walked up the road and into a lane where the inn was. Without any warning one of them slugged me from behind."

Frank said, "And put you in the blanket."

Joe said that later, as he started to come to in the inn, a drug was forced into his mouth and he was made to drink some water. He passed out, and did not wake up until morning, when they were carrying him in the blanket to their friend's saloon.

"Just as we drove out of the lane and on to the Gresham road," Joe continued, "I heard a car coming and managed to raise up. It looked like ours, so I tried to signal. Then Gross shoved me down."

Joe had been driven to Shore Road and taken to the cave through an abandoned shaft.

"You were there nearly two whole days!" Frank said.

"Most of the time I was alone. They fixed up a few sacks for me to lie on, but they didn't pay much attention to me. Once in a while they would bring in sandwiches and water and feed them to me."

"Did you find out what they're up to?" Frank asked.

"At night, when they thought I was asleep, I overheard enough to learn one of the gang's secrets. They're smugglers!"

Aunt Gertrude opened her mouth wide. "Smugglers!" she gasped. "What kind?"

"Diamonds and electronic equipment. That's probably why they wanted to get Mr Wright's special radio."

Joe paused and Mrs Hardy asked if he were too tired to go on. "No, I'm okay, Mother. I also learned that one of the top men is named Chris. From what was said, I'd guess he's that big fair-haired man who's been watching us."

Frank was excited by this news. Now they had something definite to go on! If Joe were right, they could concentrate on finding Chris and turning him over to the police.

Joe spoke up. "There are four or five in the gang working with Chris, and others offshore. Chris delivers smuggled diamonds. His pals in the cave—one tall and dark, one red-haired, and one short—mentioned that he had diamonds in his briefcase. Chris thought we had seen them when the case burst open. Gross saw a chance to kidnap one of us to keep us from talking."

"A stupid move," Frank commented. "Even if we had seen the diamonds, we wouldn't have known they'd been smuggled. What about Mr Wright's secret radio? Did they talk about that?"

"I'm not sure," Joe answered. "Gross mentioned a secret gadget, but since they smuggle electronic equipment, it could be anything. Do we still have the transistor?" he asked.

"Yes. But it's my guess someone connected with the smugglers figured out that we have the radio and thought it might be in our boot. Do you know the names of any of the others in the gang?"

Joe shook his head. "I'm sure there's a big boss, but they never mentioned him. One man who came to the cave had a nasal voice. He sounded like one of those burglars at Mr Wright's house."

"And he's afraid of someone named Shorty," Frank added. "This is a real clue." After a moment he said thoughtfully, "So we're up against a gang of smugglers."

"I think," Aunt Gertrude said firmly, "that you boys should leave well enough alone. Joe is back safe and sound, and we ought to be satisfied. If you try tracking down those smugglers, you'll only end up in trouble. Leave it to the police."

The conversation was interrupted by the ringing of the telephone. Frank answered the call.

"Are you one of the Hardy boys?" a strange voice asked.

"Yes. Who is this?"

"The inventor of the secret radio."

"What's your name?" Frank asked.

"You know I don't want to mention it on the phone. All I want to find out is whether you still have it," the man replied.

Frank was suspicious at once. He beckoned his mother and wrote on the telephone pad, *Go next door and try to have this call traced. Then call the police and give them Joe's clues to the kidnappers.*

Aloud Frank was saying, "Why are you so interested, sir?"

" 'Cause I'm the inventor and I want the radio back." The stranger spoke sharply.

A long parley followed. Finally, when Frank was sure his mother had had time to call the police, he said, "Sorry not to help you, sir, but you'll have to get your information from my father. He isn't here right this minute."

"Your father!" the man shrieked. "Why, you impudent young pup! I'll be right over and you'll give me that radio or I'll—I'll—"

The caller hung up.

·9·

Smuggler's Trail

THE evening passed with no further word from the mysterious caller who had phoned from a public booth but had disappeared before the police could track him down. Frank and Joe discussed the situation.

"Maybe he was scared off," Joe suggested. "And what about the secret radio? Somebody may look in the boot again."

"Right," Frank agreed. "I'll bring it in here. But each time we leave the house let's take the invention along."

Before the family went to bed, Mrs Hardy turned on the burglar alarm, which was connected to every door and window in the house and garage. There was no disturbance during the night.

"We're safe so far," Frank remarked at breakfast. "Maybe the police have caught Chris and the others. I'll phone Chief Collig."

"Sorry, Frank," came the report from headquarters. "None of my men has picked up a clue."

Almost a week passed. Still there was no news. The kidnapper-smugglers had covered their tracks well.

Joe had recovered from his experience and Frank's

injured leg had healed. The brothers were ready to continue their sleuthing. They asked Chet, Jerry, and Biff to help them.

"Gross and the others may sneak back to Bayport," Frank prophesied. "They'll get nervy soon and we may have a chance to trip them up."

"Where do we go from here?" Biff asked.

"A tour of the docks," Frank answered, "to hunt for a whaler."

A long but wary search of Bayport's busy waterfront yielded nothing. Finally all the boys went home.

Frank and Joe found that Aunt Gertrude had been shopping. "Who is that new young man working in Bickford's jewellery shop?" she asked abruptly.

"I never saw a *young* man working in there," Frank replied. "The only assistant I know of is elderly and he's in the hospital right now."

"A young man, I said," Aunt Gertrude repeated in a tone that did not invite contradiction. "A very suspicious-looking young man. He wasn't there the last time I went in."

"He's new to me," Joe remarked. "What happened?"

"You see this diamond pin I'm wearing?" Aunt Gertrude pointed to a small one on the shoulder of her dress. "Well, he kept eying it while I was looking at some inexpensive watches."

"He was probably just admiring it, Aunty," Frank suggested.

"Admiring it, yes. With the thought of stealing it!" Aunt Gertrude was warming to her subject. "You can't fool me about young men. Besides, I've seen that assistant somewhere before."

"Where?" Joe asked.

"I'm not sure, but I know I have seen him."

"Is that all you have against the poor fellow?" Frank asked jokingly.

"It's enough. Mark my words, that young jewellery assistant is bad. Next thing we hear of him he'll be in prison for robbing his employer!"

This dire prediction left the Hardy boys wondering. Aunt Gertrude's intuition was amazing. They would drop into Bickford's tomorrow and talk to the assistant.

The following morning the boys decided to walk downtown. They made sure their mother and aunt would be at home to guard Mr Wright's invention.

On the way Frank said, "I wonder why those smugglers operate in Bayport. Wouldn't you think they'd pick one of the larger cities?"

"Perhaps they are known in those places," Joe suggested. "I wish I could have heard more when I listened to them in the cave—like where the diamonds and electronic stuff came from and where they make their headquarters."

Suddenly Joe gripped his brother's arm. "Look!" he said tensely.

He gestured towards a man walking on the other side of the relatively deserted street and Frank almost shouted with excitement. The man was tall and muscular, with a shock of fair hair protruding from beneath his hat. He was the person who had been at the airport—the one they now suspected might be part of the kidnap-smuggler gang.

"I'll bet his name is Chris!" Frank whispered.

"Let's trail him and see where he's going."

"We'd better cross the street. He may catch sight of us."

Excitedly the Hardys hurried to the opposite side and fell in behind the fair-haired man. "Chris," apparently unaware that he was being followed, strode along at a rapid pace.

"Perhaps he's going to meet some of his pals," Joe said.

"We won't let him out of our sight," Frank said, "and if we meet a policeman I'll ask him to notify headquarters."

They were careful to remain far enough behind so that there were always several people between them and their quarry. The fair-haired man did not look back. He seemed to be in a hurry.

"You'd think Bayport has no cops," Joe complained when the boys had gone several blocks without meeting one.

The Hardys trailed the big man for several blocks. Abruptly he struck off down a side street. The boys had to run in order to keep him in sight.

"Perhaps," Joe said, "he saw you and me and is trying to shake us off."

"I don't think so. I believe he's going to the railway station."

"Good grief! If he takes a train out of town, we'll lose him."

"I don't intend to lose him," Frank declared. "How much money do you have with you?"

Joe groped in his pockets. "About seven dollars."

"Luck's with us. I have thirty. We can take the train if he does, but I hope he won't go far."

It was soon evident that Chris was indeed bound for the station. When he came in sight of the big brick building, he broke into a run and disappeared through the massive doorway.

The Hardys hastened in pursuit, still looking for a policeman. Just before reaching the station, they saw one of their father's friends. Quickly Frank told him the story and added, "Call headquarters and my mother." He dashed after Joe.

When the boys entered the station they saw Chris just leaving one of the ticket windows. He ran across to an exit, raced through it, and darted towards a waiting train.

Frank stepped up to the window which the fair-haired man had just left.

"Where to?" the agent asked.

"We wanted to meet a man here," Frank explained. "He's a big fellow with blond hair. Have you seen him?"

"Just bought a ticket to New York City a minute ago."

Frank was taken aback. He had not anticipated that Chris would be going as far as New York. However, having once picked up the trail, the young detective decided to follow it.

"Two one-way tickets," he said.

"You'll have to hurry," the agent said. "The express is due to leave right away."

Frank grabbed the tickets. He heard a whistle and saw that the train was beginning to move.

The boys dashed to the platform. Joe, in the lead, scrambled up the rear steps of the last coach. Frank followed.

When the boys had recovered their breath, they went through to the coach Chris occupied. They halted in the rear doorway and made a quick survey of the occupants.

Alone in a front seat they saw a familiar thatch of yellow hair. Chris was unaware that he had been followed,

The boys took seats at the rear of the coach, and settled down for the journey.

·10·

Elevator Chase

"I HOPE the Bayport police communicate with the authorities in New York," Frank remarked. "If they meet the train and arrest Chris, our worries will be over."

"And if they don't?" Joe asked.

Frank gave a wan smile. "Our troubles will just be starting. There'll be crowds and it'll be tough to keep track of him."

The train did not make many stops, but each time it did, Frank and Joe were ready to hop off in case Chris should alight. At length the train reached the suburbs, clattering past miles of factories and houses, and finally lurched to a halt in the underground station in New York City.

The boys watched Chris intently as the passengers prepared to leave. The fair-haired man did not look back once. He put on his hat and strolled towards the front of the coach.

"We'll get out at the back and keep an eye on him from there," Frank said.

The Hardys scrambled on to the platform where passengers were just beginning to file up the ramp to the waiting room. Chris had not yet appeared, so the brothers, shielding their faces, made their way quickly to the exit gate.

"I don't see any police," Frank remarked, disappointed.

"No," Joe replied. "I guess we'll have to take over."

The boys emerged into the concourse. There, in the enormous, high-vaulted station, booming with hollow echoes, they waited for Chris to appear.

He stalked through the gate, looking neither to right nor left. The boys quickly fell in behind him. He towered above the throng, and they had little difficulty following him. Despite the crowds that jostled them, the Hardys managed to keep Chris in view and pursued him out into the street.

"What'll we do if he hops into a taxi?" Joe asked.

"Hop into one ourselves and hope we can trail him," Frank said.

"I'd feel better if we had more money with us," Joe mumbled.

The man they were trailing still seemed unaware that he was being followed.

"It's going to be mighty hard for one taxi to follow another in this traffic," Frank remarked.

"Maybe we won't need one," his brother suggested. "Anyhow, these New York taxi drivers are pretty clever. I think if we tell one to follow a car we point out and make it worth his while, he could do it."

"Going to cost a lot of moolah," Frank said.

They were relieved when their quarry continued walking.

"Come on!" Frank called.

The two sleuths had a twofold problem: to follow

Chris and be careful he did not suspect they were after him. Twice he swung round while they hurried along the crowded sidewalk, and it seemed as if he were suspicious.

On these occasions the boys dodged behind passers-by. After two momentary surveys, Chris hastened on again.

"I don't believe he saw us," Frank murmured as they again took up the chase.

"No, evidently not. But we're coming to heavy congestion. Look at the crowd and there are traffic signals. If he gets across the street ahead of us and you and I are held up by a red light, we'll lose him."

The boys were anxious as they approached a busy corner where a policeman was directing the flow of traffic and pedestrians.

"Shall we ask his help?" Joe asked.

"I doubt if he could leave his post," Frank answered.

Just what Joe had feared took place. Chris was among the last to slip across the street before the lights flashed from green to red and the officer blew his whistle sharply. Joe groaned.

"Just our luck!" he cried.

"Look!" Frank exclaimed. "We're in luck!"

Chris was speaking to a man on the other side of the street. Evidently the stranger had asked directions and Chris had halted to explain and point out the location of a certain street. He took such pains with the man that by the time he finished, the traffic light had again flashed green.

"Let's go!" Joe cried.

They trailed Chris along the street for several blocks,

then he turned into a large office building. Inside was a row of elevators opposite the entrance. Frank and Joe hesitated for a few seconds before following Chris.

"Come on!" Joe urged. "If he gets in an elevator, and we aren't there, we won't know what office he's going to."

"You're right!" Frank agreed.

They hurried into the lobby just as Chris stepped into one of the cars. The door closed and he shot upwards. Fortunately he was the only passenger and the boys watched the dial. The lift stopped at the tenth floor.

"I hope he doesn't get away," Joe murmured excitedly.

"We never would have dared get into the same elevator with him," Frank said. "He'd have recognized us."

The boys stepped into the next lift, which soon filled up. The boys left it at the tenth floor. Each wondered if they could locate Chris in the maze of offices.

Again luck was with them. As Frank and Joe looked down a corridor, Chris was just entering an office. Evidently he had been delayed looking for his destination.

The Hardys hurried to the door as it closed behind the suspect. It was a green-painted steel door with an open transom. The sign read:

SOUTH AFRICAN IMPORTING COMPANY
WHOLESALE ONLY

"I wonder what he's doing in there," Joe murmured.

Frank put a finger to his lips. The sound of muffled voices could be heard from the office. Apparently

Chris and the others inside were so far from the door that their conversation was indistinct.

A moment later Chris's voice came loud and clear. He must be walking towards the outer door!

"We'd better scram," Frank advised.

"When he comes out, shall we grab him?" Joe asked.

Frank shook his head. "If those are buddies of his in there, they may grab *us*."

The boys scooted up the corridor and watched Chris over their shoulders. He did not notice Frank and Joe. The suspect was looking intently at some papers in his hand as he went to the elevators and pushed a button for an ascending car. He was going to a higher floor.

"Shall we follow him?" Joe whispered.

"Too risky. Let's go down and wait in the lobby, then take up the trail again."

After Chris had gone up, the boys took a down lift. On the ground floor they watched each descending elevator. After half an hour had passed, their patience was rewarded. Amid a carload of businessmen, they saw the burly form of the big blond man towering above all the others.

"Come on!" Frank whispered to Joe as Chris moved towards the street doors.

Again the chase was resumed in the crowded street. For several blocks Chris maintained a straight course. Then he swung round a corner and stalked down a side street. The sleuths hurried after their quarry and saw him dip beneath a restaurant sign below street level.

"Oh—oh!" Joe muttered. "If we follow him in there, he can't miss us."

"Let's see if there are many customers inside," Frank

suggested. "If so, we just might be able to get away with it. Could be he's meeting someone there."

Frank went down the steps leading to the restaurant and made a quick survey of the place through the door. It was almost full.

"Chris is taking a table in the rear, and he's not facing the door. Come on, Joe! We're not letting him out of our sight."

Boldly Frank and Joe entered the place. It was a cheap restaurant, with a row of booths along one side. The boys slipped quickly into one of the compartments. They could watch Chris but he could not see them.

"This is a break!" Joe whispered.

An untidy-looking waiter came over and they gave their orders. After he had gone to the kitchen, the boys put their money on the table.

"There's enough to pav for a hotel room if we have to stay over, and a few more meals."

"We can't afford to hang around New York long," Joe remarked, eyeing their available cash. "I guess we'd better tell the police about Chris and forget trying to spot his buddies."

Suddenly Frank sat bolt upright. "Chris is getting up from his table."

"Leaping lizards!" Joe exclaimed. "He's heading right for us!"

·11·

Discovered!

JOE pretended to be searching for something he had dropped and quickly ducked his head underneath the table as the fair-haired man approached. Frank snatched up a menu and held it in front of his face.

There was a tense moment as Chris drew nearer. To the boys' relief, he brushed past without noticing them and walked directly to the cashier's counter. The Hardys got ready to pursue him, but he only stopped to glance at a newspaper lying there, then returned to his own table.

"Whew, that was close!" Joe murmured as he raised his head.

"It sure was," Frank agreed. "But we have one thing in our favour. We're the last persons in the world Chris would expect to find trailing him in New York City."

The Hardys watched as a waiter walked up to the big man's table. Apparently Chris was well known in the restaurant, for the two exchanged a few words, laughing all the while. Presently a slim, sharp-featured man emerged from a door to the kitchen and went directly to Chris. He sat down, then began to talk.

"I think," Joe whispered, "it's time for some action. How about my going outside and looking for a policeman?"

"Good idea, Joe. I have a feeling the man with Chris should be investigated, too. He may be one of the smugglers."

Joe slid from the booth and went outside. No officer was in sight, but there was a public-telephone booth nearby. "I'll call headquarters from here," Joe decided and dialled the number.

He was connected with a lieutenant, who said they had been alerted by Chief Collig, but the boys' message to him had been delayed, and the call to New York had come too late for the police to meet the train from Bayport. "I will send two officers to the restaurant. If this man Chris hasn't started to eat yet, he'll be there a while. By the way, we got a message that you are to phone your home at once."

"Thank you," said Joe and hung up.

He immediately dialled the Hardy House. Aunt Gertrude answered. "My, you boys certainly take off fast! You ought to be right here taking care of the secret radio mystery."

"What do you mean, Aunty?"

"I mean that I can't understand your father. He sent a telegram saying, 'Inventor will phone. Do as directed.' Well, the inventor called and said we should leave the radio on the front steps at ten o'clock tonight."

Joe was astounded. After a moment's thought he said, "I think the telegram was a hoax. Dad would never do such a thing. Somebody may be listening in on this call, but I'll take a chance. Put a package on the steps but not the radio. Then ask the police to shadow the house and pick up this fake inventor. I have to say good-bye now. Frank and I have one of the gang almost nabbed. Give my love to Mother. Tell her we're sorry we couldn't call before this."

Joe returned to the restaurant and in whispers repeated his whole conversation. Frank nodded, then pointed to Chris's table.

"I heard that thin guy call him Chris, so we know for sure we're on the right track."

The smuggler and his companion were busily engaged with pencil and paper. Chris seemed to be explaining something that did not please the other man, for he shook his head doubtfully and crossed out what Chris had already jotted down.

"I'd give anything to know what those two are talking about," Frank said in a low tone.

"So would I," Joe replied and started to eat.

At that instant the boys' attention was diverted to a stocky man who had just entered the restaurant. He glanced in their direction, then made his way towards them. He planted himself in front of their table and glared at the Hardys.

"What's the idea of sittin' at my table?" he demanded.

"*Your* table?" Frank asked in surprise.

"Yes. This is my table you're sittin' at. You'd better clear out!"

"There are lots of other tables," Frank retorted in a low voice.

"Sure. And you can have any one of 'em you want."

Frank decided that nothing would be gained by

arguing with the stranger. Both boys returned quietly to their meal and did not look up.

"Well," the man roared, "are you gonna move?"

"As soon as we've finished our lunch," Joe snapped.

"You'll move now! This is my table you're sittin' at, and I mean to have it!"

The young sleuths were infuriated by the intrusion. Unknowingly the man was putting them in a difficult position. If they stood up to walk to another table, Chris would surely spot them and might escape before the police arrived! If they remained where they were, they probably would be discovered, since the incident was beginning to attract attention.

Frank signalled a waiter standing nearby.

"What's the trouble, Mr Melvin?" he asked.

"These kids are sittin' at my table," Melvin protested. "Make 'em move!"

The waiter looked uneasy. "I can't ask these young men to move, Mr Melvin. They were here first."

"Ain't I a good customer of this restaurant?"

"Yes, indeed. But there are plenty of other tables, sir. If you don't mind—"

"I do mind. These boys can get outta here or I won't come back to this restaurant again!" Melvin shouted.

Frank saw that Chris and his friend had turned and were looking in the Hardys' direction. At once Chris spoke to the sharp-featured man, who nodded. Then both darted towards the kitchen door and disappeared through it.

Joe said to the waiter, "We're not afraid of this fellow, but we'll leave just to save trouble."

The boys got up. Melvin, breathing defiance and

declaring that no person could sit at *his* table and get away with it, promptly sat down in the seat Frank had just vacated.

Joe dashed to the back of the restaurant and whirled into the kitchen. Chris and his friend were not in sight, but a back door was open and Joe assumed the men had ducked outside and up a delivery alley to the street. He hurried back into the restaurant.

Frank had hastened to the cashier's desk and paid the boys' bill. Then he ran up the front steps and into the street. The police had not arrived.

Joe joined his brother. "Chris left by the back door," he said. "He should be coming up that alley." When the two men did not put in an appearance, he added, "You stay here, Frank. I'll run down."

Joe returned in a short time. "Come on!" he cried, and explained that the alley joined another one that led to the busy street beyond. They followed it to the sidewalk, which was teeming with pedestrians. Chris was not in sight.

"We've really lost him this time," Joe commented in disgust.

"I have an idea," Frank said. "Let's walk along this street in opposite directions for about ten or twelve blocks. I'll head downtown, you uptown. There's a slight chance one of us might spot Chris."

"But he might have gone across town," Joe argued.

"You're right. But what have we to lose?"

"Okay, Frank, I'm game. But there's just one hitch. If I should see Chris, how do I let you know and vice versa?"

Frank looked around and pointed to a public-telephone booth. He walked over and jotted down the number.

Rejoining his brother, he said, "We'll meet back here in half an hour. However, if one of us gets back and the other isn't here, I say stay by the phone and wait for a call." He handed Joe a copy of the number and took one himself.

"Here's hoping!" Joe declared with a grin as the boys went their separate ways.

Frank walked along slowly, dividing his attention between weaving among pedestrians and searching for his quarry. When he had covered nearly fifteen blocks, Frank decided to work his way back on the opposite side of the street.

He stopped for a moment at an amusement arcade to watch the people playing the various coin-operated machines.

As Frank was about to continue walking, his eyes widened in surprise. Towards the rear of the arcade a big fair-haired man was engaged in conversation with three ominous-looking characters. Frank carefully edged his way inside the arcade for a better look. He was certain now.

The man was Chris!

·12·

Tunnel Scare

FRANK mingled with the crowd in the arcade and cautiously worked his way towards the spot where Chris and his companions were standing. He kept glancing towards the street, hoping a policeman would come along. Soon the young sleuth was close enough to overhear the men's conversation.

"Sounds like you got in with a gang that's going places," declared one of Chris's companions. "How about talkin' to your boss and gettin' us in on the action?"

"Sorry, but I can't help you guys," the fair-haired man answered. "The big boss has all the men he needs."

"Keep us in mind if anything comes up," one of the trio chimed in.

Just then a man who had been playing one of the game machines beside Frank shouted, "Whee! I've won ten in a row. I musta broke some kind o' record!"

The outburst caused Chris and his friends to look in the man's direction—and therefore right at Frank. The boy turned quickly and gazed into one of the coin-operated machines. In its highly polished surface he could see Chris's reflection.

"He must have recognized me!" Frank thought, noting a look of surprise on the smuggler's face.

Frank watched as the fair-haired man whispered something to his friends then left for the street.

Determined not to let the big man out of his sight, and to contact the first police officer he met, the young detective started off in pursuit. To his dismay, he was intercepted at the entrance by Chris's three companions.

"Where d'you think you're goin', kid?" one of them growled.

Another said, "We don't like the idea of our pal being shadowed."

"Get out of my way!" Frank demanded.

One man stepped behind the youth. The other two each grabbed an arm and led him out of the arcade.

"We're goin' for a little walk," one of them snarled, "and if you make one sound, it'll be curtains for you!"

Frank was forced to walk about half a block, then he was led into a dark, narrow alley.

"You need to be taught a lesson, kid," the man behind Frank said. "We don't like snoopers."

Frank was in a desperate situation, but he did not panic. With catlike speed he thrust out his leg and tripped the man on his right, then he flung him down so hard that the grasp on his right arm was broken. With his free arm Frank jabbed an elbow into the midriff of the man behind him.

"Ouch!" his opponent grunted loudly.

The third man, who still had a firm grip on Frank's left arm, was unable to dodge the boy's blow. It caught him on the chin and he crumpled to the ground.

Frank had only a second to collect his wits. One of his stunned opponents had recovered quickly, scrambled to his feet, and was now prepared to attack him. Just as Frank dealt the man a staggering blow, he heard a noise behind him. Before Frank could turn, he was struck on the head with a hard object.

Several minutes passed before Frank regained consciousness. He slowly got to his feet and looked around. The three men were gone. Frank grimaced as he felt a large swelling on the back of his head. Then he noticed that his wrist watch and wallet were missing.

"Chris has some rough playmates," he thought. "And they're petty thieves to boot."

Still a bit unsteady on his legs, Frank finally started uptown to rendezvous with his brother. Frank's body ached, but a light rain which was falling seemed cool and refreshing to him.

When Joe saw Frank's condition, he exclaimed, "Leaping hyenas! You look as if you'd fallen into a cement mixer!"

"Not quite," Frank replied. "I ran into some of Chris's pals."

"What! You mean you caught up with the smuggler?"

"Yes, but lost him again. I'll tell you all about it later. But first let's find some shelter from this rain. I'm cold."

They ducked into a doorway. Frank straightened his tie and brushed off his clothes in an effort to look more presentable.

"My wallet was stolen," he said. "How much money do you have left?"

Joe dug into his pockets. "Exactly six dollars and thirty-seven cents."

"I'm starved," Frank announced. "And we'll need most of that to get a good meal. Anyway, it's not enough for our fare back home. Let's find a restaurant and a phone. We can call Mother and let her know what has happened so far. Hope she can wire us some money."

The rain lessened and the boys hurried along the street in search of an eating place. They examined the menus posted in the windows of several restaurants, hoping to find one that would not exceed their budget.

"Here's a possibility," Joe said. "The menu looks good and the prices are reasonable."

The boys entered the restaurant and sat down. Shortly a waiter walked over to them. He eyed Frank's rumpled clothes and the man's manner became abrupt. The Hardys had already selected a dinner listed on the window menu and ordered immediately.

"I have a feeling he's in a hurry to get rid of us." Joe grinned as the waiter walked off.

"Did you see the way he stared at me when he came over?" Frank laughed. "I admit I look a little shabby. He probably thinks we're not going to pay our bill."

After finishing dessert, Frank rose. "Give me some change and I'll place a call home," he told Joe. "Meanwhile, you take care of the bill."

Locating a phone booth at the rear of the restaurant, the young detective deposited the coin and dialled the operator.

"I'm sorry," said a feminine voice when Frank tried to make a collect call to Bayport. "Violent storms up

there have temporarily affected the service. I suggest
you try again in about an hour."

Disappointed, Frank returned to the table. To his
surprise, Joe was involved in an argument with their
waiter.

"What's wrong?" Frank asked.

"There seems to be a misunderstanding about our
check," Joe declared. "It's almost double the amount
listed on the menu we saw in the window."

"I already told you," the waiter growled. "Those
prices are good only up to three o'clock. After that, you
pay more."

"I'll say you do," Joe retorted. "But how were we
supposed to know?"

The waiter picked up a copy of the menu the boys
had seen in the window and thrust it at them. "Can't
you read?" He pointed to a line of fine print at the
bottom of the menu:

> THIS MANAGEMENT RESERVES THE
> PRIVILEGE TO CHANGE LISTED MENU
> PRICES AFTER THREE P.M.

"Wow! You almost need a magnifying glass to read
it!" Joe snapped.

"Don't try to squirm out of this," the waiter said
harshly. "I had you kids sized up the minute you
walked in here. I'm going to get the manager!"

The waiter reappeared shortly with a short, stocky
man wearing a dark suit and a bow tie.

"I hear you boys can't pay your bill," he said.

Joe started to explain. "We can pay you half of it
now and . . ."

"We don't sell meals on the instalment plan," the manager stated tersely.

"Give us a little time," Frank pleaded. "Just as soon as we can get a call through to our home, we'll have some money wired."

"A lot of good that will do me," the manager answered. Suddenly his expression changed. His face broke into a wide grin. "Tell you what! I'm in need of a couple of dishwashers right now. Each of you work for three hours and I'll call it square. You keep your money."

The Hardys were reluctant, but being short on funds, with no place to go, and unable to get through to Mrs Hardy yet, they agreed.

After working a while Joe said in disgust, "A couple of private detectives end up in New York as kitchen police!"

"I wouldn't complain too much," Frank said, grinning. "What if we had to wash these dishes by hand!"

"Why do we have to do them at all?" Joe complained. "Dad has several friends here in the city. They'd be willing to help us out with some money."

"I know! But I think we should go to them only as a last resort."

Frank waited nearly four hours before getting a call through to Bayport. Finally the lines were repaired, and a long-distance operator connected him with Mrs Hardy.

"Your Aunt Gertrude and I have been worried sick about you and Joe," she said. "There's been a bad storm here. Where *are* you?"

"Still in New York. But guess what? Joe and I are washing dishes to pay for our dinner."

Mrs Hardy laughed and promised to wire them money right away.

"Send it to the telegraph office at Grand Central Terminal," Frank requested. "And don't worry about us. We're fine, and we'll probably be home tomorrow. Now tell me, did that fake inventor show up?"

"No. I guess the storm was too bad. The detectives stationed here were needed elsewhere and had to leave. The box on the steps is soaked. We turned the lights off and have been watching from the window. Maybe we can catch a glimpse of whoever comes."

"Good. 'Bye now. I hope nobody tapped this call."

When Frank and Joe finished their work, they hurried from the restaurant. It was still raining when they stepped on to the street. "It's almost midnight. What now?" Joe asked.

"Let's take the subway to Times Square," Frank said. "Then we can get the cross-town shuttle train to Grand Central. At least we can keep dry there until our money arrives."

There were only a few people waiting for the shuttle train when the boys arrived at Times Square. Several minutes passed, then suddenly Frank clutched his brother's arm.

"What's the matter?" Joe asked.

"That man behind the post!" Frank whispered. "He's one of Chris's friends!"

Just as Joe glanced up, the man brushed against one of the strolling passengers on the platform. The young detectives' keen eyes saw him lift a wallet from his victim's pocket.

"Hey! You!" Frank shouted, rushing towards the pickpocket with Joe close behind him.

Startled at Frank's outcry, the thief quickly removed the money and dropped the wallet. He leaped off the platform on to the tracks and disappeared into the dark tunnel. The boys took off in pursuit.

"Watch that side rail!" Frank warned his brother. "It's charged with high-voltage electricity!"

The young detectives had run a considerable distance into the yawning tunnel when they halted abruptly.

"What's that rumbling noise?" Joe asked.

"It's the shuttle train!" Frank screamed. "And it's coming our way!"

Seconds later the fast-moving train loomed round the bend. Would the Hardys escape in time?

·13·

Exciting Assignment

"RUN for it!" Joe yelled.

The boys whirled and dashed through the tunnel. As the train rapidly gained on them, its headlight illuminated the walls. Stretching along one side was a power line encased in metal piping. Frank spotted it.

"That's a conduit line!" he shouted. "Grab it and flatten yourself against the wall!"

They made a desperate leap, caught hold of the narrow piping, and stiffened themselves hard against the wall. Seconds later the train sped past them. The roar was deafening and the mass of air that was pulled along lashed the Hardys like a gale. The sides of the carriages were barely inches away as the lighted windows passed by in a blur.

Soon the last coach disappeared round a bend. The youths jumped on to the tracks and made their way back to the Times Square station platform. Both were trembling.

"What do you think happened to the man we were chasing?" Joe asked finally.

"Probably he's used this tunnel before as a means of escape," Frank replied, "and knows the layout well. I'm sure he's heading for Grand Central station."

Arriving at the platform, the boys spotted the man Chris's pal had tried to rob. He was talking to a police officer.

"These are the two boys who chased the pickpocket into the tunnel," the man told the policeman as the brothers walked towards them.

The officer turned to Frank and Joe. "This man claims someone stole his wallet."

"That's right," Frank said, "and the thief is probably the same one who lifted mine this afternoon. We chased him but he got away."

"By now he has no doubt reached Grand Central," Joe added.

"I've alerted a couple of the men on duty there," the policeman said. "They'll be on the lookout for him." He stared at the boys curiously. "Say, that was a risky job for you fellows to take on!"

The boys introduced themselves to the officer and showed him their credentials.

"So you're the Hardys," the policeman remarked. "I'm Reilly. Your father's name is something of a legend round the department."

"Dad is a great detective," Joe said proudly.

At the officer's request, the boys gave him a description of the pickpocket. Reilly then took the name and address of the man who had been robbed.

Shortly the next train arrived and the Hardys stepped aboard. When they got off at Grand Central station, Frank and Joe noticed a commotion at the far end of the platform. A group of spectators had assembled.

"Let's see what's going on," Frank suggested.

As the boys walked forward, Joe's eyes widened. "Hey, look!" he yelled. "There's the pickpocket we chased!"

"He's being questioned by two policemen," Frank observed. "That was quick work. They must've nabbed him coming out of the tunnel."

The boys pressed their way through the spectators.

"I ain't done nothin'," they heard the pickpocket snarl.

"That's not true!" Joe declared. "He tried to steal a man's wallet. My brother and I saw the whole thing!"

"And I suspect he took mine and is a pal of some smugglers," Frank added.

"Who are you?" one of the policemen asked.

The boys identified themselves once more, then related the incident at the Times Square station.

One of the officers nodded. "We were alerted to be on the lookout for this guy."

"We know all about him," the second policeman said. "His name is Torchy Murks. Has two convictions for petty larceny. We had reports of a pickpocket that looks like him working the subways recently."

"You're crazy!" Murks growled. "I'm being framed!"

"We'll see about that."

The officers requested the boys to accompany them. At the police station Murks was marched off to the interrogation room.

A few minutes later a tall, muscular, square-jawed man emerged from the squad room. He walked directly to the Hardys and extended his hand in greeting.

"One of the officers has just told me that you're the sons of Fenton Hardy," he said.

"That's right."

"It's a pleasure to meet you. I'm Detective Lieutenant Danson. I joined the force as a rookie just before your father left the department. A great detective. Come into my office."

The youths were ushered into a small but comfortable office, where Danson offered them chairs and seated himself behind his desk.

"I hear you fellows had a scrap with Torchy Murks," he said. "Slippery character. Well, tell me, what brings the famous Hardys to New York City?"

The boys related their experiences of the past two weeks, ending with an account of how they had trailed the smuggler-kidnapper Chris to New York.

Lieutenant Danson sat thoughtfully for several moments. "That's strange," he mumbled to himself.

"What is?" Joe inquired curiously.

"It might be just a coincidence," Danson muttered. "Then again . . ."

The boys watched with interest as the lieutenant thumbed through his private list of telephone numbers. "An FBI agent I know, named Emery Keith, dropped into my office a couple of days ago and told me about two suspects his office wants for questioning. From his description of the men, one of them sounds like this big blond fellow Chris. Of course our men have been on the lookout, but I'd like Keith to hear your story."

Twenty minutes later two neatly dressed men arrived at the lieutenant's office.

"I'm Agent Keith," the tall, light-haired one said to the Hardys. Then he introduced his shorter, dark-haired companion. "And this is my assistant, George

Mallett. I've heard a lot about your father. Some of our agents have worked with him."

After the formalities, they all sat down to discuss the case. Frank and Joe told their story about the kidnapping and smuggling.

"Hmm!" Keith muttered. "Interesting lead!" The agent eyed the Hardys for a moment before speaking again. "Does the name Taffy Marr ring a bell with you fellows?" he asked.

"I'm afraid not," Frank replied.

"Taffy Marr," Keith said, "is one of the slickest crooks in the country. He's the leader of the smuggling ring and I suspect is the boss of Shorty, Chris, and their pals. Marr is young—the innocent-looking type—but as clever and cold-blooded a crook as you'll ever come up against."

"What else can you tell us about his looks?" Frank asked.

"Not much. Taffy is slender, of average height, and uses a lot of disguises, so we're not exactly sure what he does look like. One of our men did spot a triangular scar on Marr's left forearm. No doubt he's self-conscious about this identification and he usually wears long sleeves.

"Taffy came from the West Coast a few months ago and organized a gang," Keith went on. "The group's been flooding the country with smuggled diamonds. It's so bad that the Jewellers Association is offering a sizeable reward to anyone who can trip up Marr. As for me, I'd give a year's salary to put him in prison."

Joe volunteered the information that the gang also

smuggled electronic equipment, and added, "Have you any leads on Marr's whereabouts?"

"The last report shows he was here in New York," the agent answered. "Before that, it was Florida, then Virginia, Connecticut, New Jersey, and the Carolinas."

"He certainly gets around," Frank commented.

"Apparently he's confining his operations now to the East Coast," Keith said. "But the problem is where. He has dropped out of sight completely."

"How long do you two plan to be in New York?" Keith asked the Hardys.

"Not much longer," Joe said. "We called home for money, and it should be at the Grand Central telegraph office by now. We plan to take the first train back to Bayport."

"Tell you what," Keith said. "Why not let us put you up at a hotel tonight at our expense? Then you can catch the morning train. I'd like to have breakfast with you fellows and discuss the possibility of your working with us. But I'll have to talk with my chief first."

Frank and Joe were excited at this prospect and quickly consented. Lieutenant Danson drove them to Grand Central, where they found their money waiting, then they went to a nearby hotel. Completely exhausted, Frank and Joe were sound asleep within minutes.

Early the next morning they met Keith in the hotel restaurant and enjoyed a breakfast of sausage, wheat cakes, and fruit. Then the agent reviewed the facts on Marr and his gang.

"I realize our information is sketchy," the agent said. "But you've given us some good leads and maybe you can dig up a few more."

"We'll certainly try," Frank said.

"I'd like you fellows to be on the lookout for Marr in the Bayport area. The same goes for Chris. He may turn up there again—perhaps to meet Marr, if they're in the same racket."

"You can count on us!" Joe said eagerly.

Keith reached into his pocket and took out a small business card. On the back he jotted down a series of digits.

"I suggest you memorize this telephone number," he said. "You'll be able to get in touch with me or my assistant Mallet at any time."

"Right!" The Hardys repeated the digits several times until both were sure they would not forget them.

Frank telephoned to check the trains and learned that one would depart for Bayport within half an hour. Keith drove them to the station and shook hands.

"Good luck, and good hunting," he said with a smile. "I can assure you that the entire Bureau will be grateful for whatever help you can give it."

When the boys arrived home, Joe jokingly stuck out his chest and said to Mrs Hardy and Aunt Gertrude, "Meet a couple of Federal men!"

"Whatever do you mean?" his mother asked.

Frank told of Keith's request and the women smiled. "It's a big assignment," Mrs Hardy remarked, and Aunt Gertrude added, "You'd better watch your step. This Marr fellow sounds pretty dangerous for you to tackle."

"Now tell us," Joe requested, changing the subject, "about that fake inventor. Did the mysterious caller ever come for the box with the secret radio in it?"

"Yes," their mother replied.

"Was he caught?" Frank asked eagerly.

·14·

Identification Diamond

AUNT Gertrude answered Frank's question. "Of course that crook was caught. The police came back and nabbed him. Inventor, nothing."

"Hurrah!" Joe shouted. "Who is he?"

"He won't talk and he had no identification on him. But I'll bet he belongs to Chris's gang," Miss Hardy said.

"You're probably right," Frank agreed. "And they may all belong to Marr's racket." After a few moments' thought, he added, "I think I know a way to find out."

"How?" Joe asked.

Frank grinned. "I'll pretend I'm a fellow gang member and go and talk to him."

The young detective telephoned Chief Collig, who gave his consent to the plan.

"What can you tell me about this man?" Frank asked.

Hearing that the prisoner was very short and strong, Frank instantly thought of the man the burglars at the Wright home had mentioned.

"Sounds like Shorty," he said. After hanging up, he asked Mrs Hardy, "Have you an unmounted diamond?"

"Yes. One that fell out of a ring. Why?"

"I'd like to borrow one as a sort of identification with the gang."

"Swell idea," said Joe. "I'll help you get fixed up." The boys went upstairs and rummaged through their father's supply of disguises.

When Frank emerged from the house, his best friends would not have recognized him. He wore a long cut wig and beard, tight-fitting slacks, and a turtleneck sweater. He roared off on his motorcycle, and on purpose went past the cell block.

As prearranged, Chief Collig met him at the entrance to headquarters and escorted Frank to the prisoner, who looked idly through the bars.

"Friend of yours to see you," said the chief. "Maybe he can persuade you to unbutton your lips."

Frank gazed through the bars. "Like nuttin' I will," he whispered to the prisoner in a tough voice as soon as Collig had moved off. "Hi, Shorty! I'm sorry the cops got yuh. But yuh didn't tell 'em nuttin', did yuh?"

"Naw."

Frank was jubilant. He had scored one point. The man's nickname *was* Shorty.

"Did yuh hear my new motorcycle?" he asked.

"Yeah, I heard it," Shorty answered. "Whaddaya pay for it with?"

Frank pulled the diamond from his pocket. "With some o' dese."

Shorty seemed impressed. "Say, what's yer name?"

Frank assumed an air of annoyance. "Ain't Taffy told yuh 'bout me yet?"

"Naw."

The young sleuth's heart was thumping with excitement as he said, "Name's Youngster. I got a bonus on the last haul. Just joined up with Marr—when *smacko!* —I run into *the* toughest setup."

Shorty, apparently convinced by Frank's story, said, "I was lookin' fer some chips, too. But Marr'll probably have me rubbed out for gettin' in here."

"Did the cops take the Hardys' package from yuh?" Frank asked.

"Yeah. Before I could open it."

"How'd yuh like me to lift it? I could do it easy," Frank boasted.

"From the cops?" Shorty asked, astonished.

"Naw. The Hardys. The chief'll give it back to 'em."

Shorty's thin lips broke into a smile. "Then Taffy'll think I didn't bungle after all?" His face clouded again, however. "Lessen yuh double-cross me," he added.

"I won't squeal," Frank said. "I'll tell Marr yuh give it to me to deliver. Say, where's he holin' up now? I seen him in New York an' he told me to come here an' wait till I heard from him."

"Guess he's still at Bickford's," Shorty answered, and added with a smirk, "Best place to hide out with a wad o' rocks."

At that moment a voice called, "Time's up for visitors." A guard came in Frank's direction.

"Okay, but don't rush me," the elated boy said in a tough voice.

He swaggered out of the police station and walked towards his motorcycle. What should he do now? Divulge the information to Collig at once and have the police pick up Taffy Marr?

"I'll call him, anyway," Frank decided, "and he can notify Keith."

Collig said he would stake plain clothesmen at the shop. "I'll let you know what happens."

When Frank reached home, Aunt Gertrude met him at the door. "I'm glad you've come," she said excitedly. "We must do something at once about that young clerk at Bickford's."

"We are going to," her nephew assured her. "That is, the police are."

"Well, I can tell them something," Aunt Gertrude said. "I was going to tell you what I remembered about him."

"You know something about him?" Frank asked.

"I'll say I do. You recall the tall, fair-haired man who bumped into me at the Gresham railroad station and called me an old whaler? Well, it suddenly came to me that one of the men he was talking to was the very same young man who's working at Bickford's!"

"What!" Frank exclaimed. "You're sure?"

"Now listen here," his aunt said sharply. "When I'm sure, I'm sure."

"Aunty, this is great news!" Frank exclaimed.

Her announcement changed the whole scheme of attack. "Does Joe know about this and where is he?" Frank asked.

"He hasn't heard my story because I just remembered. Joe went— Here he comes now."

As Joe came in, he asked, "Frank, how did you make out?"

"Great! Listen! Taffy Marr is working at Bickford's!"

"No kidding?"

"It's straight. I got the tip from Shorty, the prisoner," Frank answered. "And listen to this. Aunt Gertrude saw Marr with Chris in Gresham! While I remove my disguise, will you call Chief Collig and tell him this?"

"Okay, and let's go down and watch the fun when Marr is arrested," Joe urged.

It took Frank only five minutes to take off his costume and make-up. Since Mrs Hardy and Aunt Gertrude planned to leave the house, Joe put Mr Wright's invention in the tyre well of the boys' car. Then he and Frank rode downtown in the convertible. When they reached Bickford's, there was a good-sized crowd in front of the jewellery store.

"What's going on?" Joe asked a bystander.

"Don't know. An attempted holdup, I guess. Police arrived and circled the building. We've been waiting for them to bring somebody out."

A siren began to wail and seconds later an ambulance raced up the street. It stopped in front of the jewellery store. A hush fell over the crowd as they waited for the victim to be brought out. Would it be Taffy Marr, or a policeman who had gone in to arrest him or would it be the shop owner?

A stretcher was carried in and a little later it was brought out bearing a man. His eyes were closed and his face ghostly white.

"It's Mr Bickford!" Joe exclaimed.

Instantly the boys pushed through the crowd and rushed up to an officer just emerging from the store. He knew the Hardys and beckoned to them.

"We were just a little too late arriving to catch

Marr," he said. "Marr must have attacked Mr Bickford and cleaned the place out before he skipped."

"A complete haul, you mean?" Joe asked.

"Took everything."

"How bad is Mr Bickford?" Frank inquired.

The officer shrugged. "He's unconscious and his pulse is weak."

Joe spluttered angrily, "If I get my hands on Marr, I'll—I'll—"

"It's going to be tough tracking him down," Frank predicted. "I'll bet by this time he's wearing a disguise and has already left town."

Joe snapped his fingers. "If he owns a suitcase full of disguises, he probably went back to wherever he's living to pick them up. Officer, have you any idea where he's living?"

"No, but our men are questioning people in the neighbourhood."

As the ambulance pulled away, the boys asked permission to check out the jewellery shop for a clue to Marr's address.

The officer smiled. "Go ahead. You fellows may manage to pick up a lead before the police check. I'm to stay on duty outside so take all the time you want."

Frank told his brother he was sure Mr Bickford would have some kind of record concerning his assistant.

"No doubt they will be under an assumed name, but let's have a look."

The boys found a drawer full of papers. Under them was an account book. They read each name listed in the book and at last came to one with recent, regular notations of payments.

"This might be him," Frank observed. "Ray Stokeley, 49 New Street."

"It's worth following," Joe said.

Frank and Joe briefly told the officer on duty they might have a lead and dashed off to their car. They soon reached New Street, where most of the old-fashioned houses had "Rooms for Rent" signs in windows. Number 49 was a large run-down mansion, set far back from the street.

Frank and Joe climbed the high steps and rang the bell. A neatly dressed, middle-aged woman opened the door.

"Is Mr Stokeley at home?" Frank inquired.

"No, he left—moved out, not ten minutes ago."

The woman started to close the door, but Frank, smiling at her, said, "We think he's the man we're looking for, but we're not sure. Would you mind describing Mr Stokeley for us?"

Her description fitted Marr. Frank nodded. "He's our man. Do you know where he went?"

There was no answer for a few seconds, then the woman said jokingly, "Who are you? Boy detectives?"

"Yes," Joe replied promptly, "and Mr Stokeley is wanted by the FBI and police. You'd be doing them a great favour if you tell us all you know."

"Oh!" she gasped. "I know very little about Mr Stokeley. But I did hear part of a phone call he made early this morning. He said, 'Then to the airport.' Does that help you?"

"Yes indeed. Thanks," Frank answered as he and Joe raced down the steps.

They arrived at the airport in record time. As they

rushed through the terminal lobby, the boys caught sight of Cole Weber, the pilot, looking at the antique aircraft and waved.

"If Marr's wearing a disguise, how can we spot him?" Frank said.

Joe was staring at a man with grey hair, moustache, and a beard. He stood near a counter, talking to a red-haired fellow.

"Frank, look! That guy the grey-haired man's talking to looks like one of the kidnappers!"

"Sure?"

"Positive! And I'll bet Grey Beard is Taffy Marr!"

The men turned and went out to the field. Frank and Joe followed. The suspects started running towards a small white single-engine plane that was ready for take-off. They climbed aboard quickly.

"Now what'll we do?" Frank asked.

"Only one thing we can do," Joe replied. "Follow them!"

·15·

Pursuit

"But how can we follow Marr?" Frank asked. "If only Dad's plane were here, we could do it easily."

He was referring to the sleek, six-seater aircraft owned by their father. However, Mr Hardy and his pilot Jack Wayne had flown it to California with Mr Wright.

"Keep an eye on that white bird," Joe ordered. "I'll run into the administration building and telephone Agent Keith. Then I'll go to Manson's Charter Service and see if we can rent a plane."

"You'd better make it quick!" Frank warned.

Joe rushed to a phone booth inside the administration building and dialled Keith's code number. It took only seconds to make the connection.

"Agent Mallett speaking!" crackled a deep, firm voice.

"This is Joe Hardy. Is Agent Keith there?"

"No, but he should be back in a few minutes."

"Can't wait!" Joe declared. "Tell him my brother and I are trailing a man we're sure is Taffy Marr. We're at Bayport field. The suspect and another man are about to take off in a white single-engine job. We'll try to follow them. I'll keep you posted!"

"Good work!" Mallett said. "Try to get the registration number of their plane so that we can trace its owner."

"Right!"

Joe hung up quickly and went directly to one of the terminal's counters. Behind it stood a plumpish, pleasant-faced man. On the wall hung a sign which read:

Manson's Charter Service

"Well, if it isn't Joe Hardy!" the man declared.

"Hello, Mr Manson."

"Where have you been keeping yourself? Haven't seen you around the airport lately."

"We've been sleuthing," Joe answered with a wink. "I'd like to charter one of your planes right away!"

"Gosh, Joe, I'm sorry, but all my aircraft are out on flights," Manson said apologetically. "Haven't had such a busy day in months."

Suddenly Joe had an idea. How about Cole Weber? He rushed off and in a few moments found the lanky owner of an antique plane.

"Nice to see you again," the pilot greeted him. "What's the rush?"

"I'm looking for a ride."

"You've come to the right man. I'll be glad to fly you wherever you want to go," Weber told him.

Joe drew the pilot aside and in a low voice briefly explained the situation to him. "Could your aircraft keep up with a fast plane?"

Frank rushed into the lobby. "Marr and his friend are getting ready to take off!" he exclaimed.

Followed by his brother and Weber, Joe ran to a window overlooking the field. They spotted the small, single-engine plane taxiing to the active runway for take-off. Frank jotted down the registration number.

"Is this the one you want to follow?" Weber commented. "That type isn't too fast. I'm sure I could keep up with it."

"Great!" said Frank.

"We'll have to make it snappy!" Joe urged.

"Maybe not," Weber answered. "There's a long line of planes waiting for take-off clearance. It'll be at least ten minutes before those men can clear ground. That'll give me time to telephone the control tower. Since my plane is not equipped with radio, they'll have to okay me for take-off by flashing a green light."

Frank said, "How about warning the control tower not to let Marr take off?"

Weber looked surprised. "Are you completely sure that one of those passengers is Marr?" he asked.

"Well, no, we're not," Joe confessed.

"Then I think we'd better not make such a request," the pilot advised. "All of us might get into trouble."

The boys nodded and Joe said, "We'll just make a chase of it."

Weber went off but soon returned. "Everything's set," he said. "And we're in luck! The control-tower boys are going to let us take off from the grass shoulder of Runway Six. It means we won't have to wait in line for clearance. Chances are we'll be off the ground ahead of your friends."

The Hardys followed the pilot to his orange-and-white biplane. He drew three parachutes from the baggage compartment and instructed Frank and Joe to put them on while he fastened his own.

"Climb aboard!" he said.

The boys seated themselves side by side in the front cockpit. Weber signalled a mechanic to help start the engine, then jumped into the rear cockpit.

"Brakes on! Contact!" the mechanic shouted.

"Brakes on! Contact!" Weber replied.

With a single whirl of the propeller, the engine roared to life. The boys were so thrilled by the chance to fly in an old biplane that for a moment they had almost dismissed Taffy Marr from their minds.

Weber began to glide his wood-and-fabric craft down the runway. Nearing Runway Six, he veered on to the grass shoulder which paralleled it.

"All set?" the boys heard him shout over the sound of the engine.

"All set!" Frank and Joe answered.

Their pilot pivoted the craft round and pointed its nose into the wind. Shortly a bright disc of green light beamed from the control tower. The engine emitted a loud, steady roar as Weber advanced the throttle. The plane bounced across the grass surface, then cleared it. Frank looked down and spotted Marr's craft just taxiing into position for take-off.

After reaching a couple of thousand feet, Weber circled the airport. He and the Hardys watched intently as the other plane sped down the runway and became airborne far below them.

Weber manœuvred his craft at a safe distance behind Marr's plane, which was now heading on a north-easterly course.

"So far so good!" Frank exclaimed, noting that their quarry was not outdistancing them. The boys waved happily to Weber, who responded with a wide grin.

Nearly half an hour had passed when they noticed a build-up of haze ahead. It seemed to thicken as they drew closer. Soon the antique craft was skirting an ocean of milky-white mist which obscured the country-side below.

"What a cloud!" Joe shouted.

"And we'll head right into it on our present course!" Frank observed.

Weber signalled that he would try flying above it. By now Marr's plane was also climbing. To the Hardys' dismay, their quarry vanished behind a screen of whiteness.

Weber signalled that he was going to turn back. But as he banked the biplane, it suddenly plunged into a misty void!

·16·

Bail Out!

WEBER struggled to keep the aircraft under control in the fog. He shifted his attention to the *turn-and-bank* indicator mounted on the instrument panel. What the dial showed would help prevent the pilot from rolling into an uncontrollable spiral.

Then, suddenly, the plane broke out into a cavity of clear air. The boys spotted the other aircraft and saw that it had altered its course. It was now heading south. Weber immediately banked and took the same direction, hoping to close the gap and come in on the tail of the other plane.

It was then that the Hardys realized the extent of the fog bank. Already obscuring a great area of the coast, it stretched far out to sea. Ahead they saw their quarry flying directly towards a looming wall of thick mist.

Weber altered course again and headed north-west in an effort to skirt the edge of the fog bank. But the mist built up rapidly in swirling clouds.

"I guess if we hope to keep the other plane in sight, we can't go too far to the west," Frank observed.

Weber began to climb, hoping to get above the fog. But as he turned north to meet the advancing cloud, his craft was enveloped in mist before he could gain altitude. Marr's plane had vanished.

"The other ship is equipped to fly on instruments!" Weber shouted. "We're not!"

Their pilot held to a straight course and increased his speed, hoping to run through the fog and pick up the other plane when visibility improved. The great bank of mist evidently extended over a greater area than he had first supposed.

Minutes ticked by and still the opaque greyness persisted. Frank and Joe turned to watch the pilot. Weber was peering at the instrument panel.

"At least we're flying straight and level," he announced.

Frank and Joe tried to remain calm but inwardly they were worried. Their craft might ram another plane at any moment!

Weber continued on into the limitless white wall. Not a glimpse of blue sky. Not a patch of earth to be seen.

"I guess we've lost Marr for sure," Joe remarked.

"Yes," Frank agreed. His voice showed his disappointment.

Suddenly the roar of the engine stopped. The only sound was the hum of the rigging. The nose of the plane dropped sharply and the craft went into a dive.

"The engine's stopped!" Joe yelled.

The pilot waved at them in an encouraging gesture. He had thrust the stick far forward and the plane was plunging through the fog at terrific speed.

On and on it went. The boys were alarmed. They knew engine trouble had developed and a forced landing in the fog would be perilous. But there must still be some hope; otherwise their pilot would have signalled to abandon ship.

The rush of air took their breath away. Then, as abruptly as it had ceased, the roar of the engine broke out again.

"Boy, what a welcome sound!" Joe exclaimed.

Weber eased the stick back slowly and the plane gradually recovered from the dive. It flattened out and began to climb again. Frank took a deep breath. Joe grinned.

But their relief was short-lived. Again the engine began to act up. It spluttered, balked, misfired, and picked up again. No longer was it throbbing with its previous regularity.

The boys looked back at the pilot's anxious face. They all knew a blind landing could be disastrous! For a moment the Hardys stiffened as the engine died, then coughed once more.

"Carburettor ice, I'll bet," Frank said to himself.

The plane they had been pursuing was forgotten. Their whole concern now was safety—to escape the grey blanket. If only they could sight ground to attempt a forced landing!

Frank felt for the harness of his parachute. "We may have to jump," he thought, not relishing the prospect. To leap from a crippled plane, with fog blanketing the earth below, was an experience he could do without.

Joe was alarmed too. "If only the fog would lift!"

The pilot was desperately trying to revive the engine's old steady clamour. But it was useless.

The engine stopped again. The nose of the machine

dropped and the plane repeated a long, swift dive. It straightened out, banked, then dived again at screaming speed.

Coming out of the second dive, the nose rose abruptly. They all waited for the reassuring catch of the engine but it remained mute.

The speed gained in the dive steadily decreased as the craft soared upwards in a steep climb. Then it fell off on one wing and went into a descending spiral.

"I have a feeling we're going in circles!" Joe shouted to his brother. "I think Weber is becoming disoriented."

"We're sunk!" Weber yelled at the boys. "You'll have to take to the chutes!"

"Jump?" Joe shouted.

The man nodded. "The engine is done for. Choked up. I don't dare try a landing in this fog. We'll crack up for sure. Hurry! I'll keep her under control as long as I can. Crawl out on the wing, watch for my signal, then jump clear! Count ten, then yank the rip cord!"

The boys scrambled out on the swaying wing in dead silence as the plane coasted through the grey mist.

"Jump clear!" Frank reminded his brother.

"It's not the jumping that worries me," said Joe. "It's the landing."

The boys knew that they had no control over their direction and had no idea of what lay beneath. They might be plunging directly towards a lake or into a city street!

Out on the wing Frank and Joe clung for a moment, their eyes on the pilot. Weber raised his hand, then brought it down sharply.

"Jump!"

Since the parachutes could easily become entangled if the boys jumped together, Frank went first. He leaped away from the swaying plane and plummeted through the fog. Then Joe followed suit.

Twisting and turning through the air, the boys plunged towards the earth. Desperately Frank groped for the rip-cord. It eluded his grasp. Sudden panic gripped him.

He was falling towards the earth at terrific speed and could not find the parachute's Dee ring!

Every second was precious. He knew that even if he found the ring, it would be a few moments before the parachute opened. By then he might already have reached an altitude too low to permit the chute to billow out in time!

His groping hand found the ring and he tugged. Nothing happened. He was still tumbling through the clouds of mist!

About to give up hope, Frank heard a crackling sound above him. There was a sudden jerk as though a gigantic hand had grabbed him and he found himself floating gently through space.

Through the wreaths of mist he glimpsed another object. It was a parachute similar to his own, dropping slowly through the fog. Joe, at least, was safe.

But what of the pilot and the crippled plane? Where were they?

The Trapped Pilot

FEAR gripping them, the Hardys drifted down silently through the fog. The only sound was an occasional flapping of the canopies looming above their heads.

"The ground can't be too far below!" Frank thought. "What kind of terrain? Sharp rocks? Trees? Open water?"

He and Joe heard a muffled explosion some distance away.

"Weber's biplane must have crashed!" Joe concluded. "Hope he bailed out in time."

Suddenly the milky void vanished. The Hardys blinked in relief. They were less than a hundred feet above a farmland area.

They settled down in a ploughed field a short distance from each other. Frank tumbled across the soft ground a couple of times, then hauled in a section of shroud lines to spill the air from the canopy of his chute.

"You all right?" he shouted to Joe, throwing off his harness and running towards him.

"I'm okay! That was wild! But I wouldn't want to do it again under the same conditions!"

Frank pointed to a plume of smoke rising behind a hill about half a mile away.

"That must be the explosion!" he yelled. "Let's see if it's Weber's plane."

They raced towards the spot. In a few minutes they came to a charred, twisted mass of wreckage. A pool of oil still burned.

"At least Weber wasn't in the wreck," said Joe. "But where is he?"

At that instant the pilot called out to them. "Hey, fellows!" he shouted. "Give me a hand!"

The voice seemed to come from a small clump of trees located about five hundred feet away. When the boys reached it, they saw Weber dangling in his harness high among some branches.

"Are you hurt?" Joe asked with concern.

"No—only my pride," the pilot answered. "I'm supposed to be an expert at handling a parachute. And where do I land and get trapped? In the only grove of trees within a mile!"

"You're too far above the ground to try dropping free," Frank warned. "We'd better get help."

People from the surrounding farms who had seen the smoke began to arrive at the scene. When the boys asked for some rope, one of the farmers rushed off. He returned in a few minutes with a coil of one-inch hemp.

Joe took it and began shinning up the tree in which Weber's chute was entangled. Everyone watched the rescue as he edged out along a branch directly above the pilot and tied one end of the rope to it. Seconds later they both were sliding to the ground.

The farmer on whose property they had landed stepped up. "My name is Hank Olsen," he said. "Was anybody injured?"

*People from the surrounding farms began to arrive
at the scene*

"No," Frank replied. "Sorry about the plane coming down on your land."

"That's all right. I haven't done any planting in that section yet," the farmer explained.

Weber spoke up. "I'd like to telephone a report of the crash."

"You can use the phone at my house," Olsen offered. "I'll drive you there. My pickup truck is just on the other side of the hill."

When they arrived at the farmhouse, the pilot called the control tower at Bayport field to report the accident. Frank phoned Mrs Hardy to let her know where he and Joe were, and then got in touch with Chet Morton for a ride home.

"What!" Chet exclaimed in disbelief when he heard about the Hardys' adventure. "Say that again."

"I said we had to bail out of Weber's biplane," Frank declared.

"Aw, come on," his chum muttered, unbelieving.

"It's true," Frank replied. "We need a ride home. Do you think your jalopy would hang together long enough for you to pick us up?"

"Hang together?" Chet retorted. "That's no way to talk about one of the finest pieces of machinery going. Where are you?"

Frank asked the farmer for their exact location. Olsen unfolded a road map and pointed to a spot about ninety miles north-east of Bayport. Frank traced the route with his finger and relayed instructions to his friend.

"Okay! I'm on my way!" Chet answered.

Nearly three hours passed before the Hardys

spotted their chum's yellow jalopy bouncing along the narrow road leading to Olsen's house. Weber and the boys thanked the farmer and his wife for their hospitality, then started for Bayport.

As they rode along, the Hardys and Weber discussed their pursuit of Marr's plane. "I wonder if he ran into any trouble," Joe mused.

"When I called control tower, I asked if they knew about the stretch of fog north of them," Weber explained. "They did, and said it was only two or three miles across, with clear air on the other side."

"And since Marr's plane was equipped with radio," Frank interrupted, "the pilot would have received the latest weather reports. He knew he could fly through the fog bank and be in the clear again within a few minutes."

"Do you think Marr knew he was being followed?" Joe asked.

"My guess is that he didn't," Weber said. "At least his pilot wasn't attempting any evasive action."

"Sorry about your plane," Joe said sympathetically.

"It was a great ship," Weber declared sadly. "But I have enough parts to rebuild another one. That's some consolation."

Chet dropped off Weber and the Hardys at Bayport field, where the pilot made arrangements to fly home. After expressing their thanks to him for his help and saying good-bye, the boys walked towards their car.

"We'd better call Agent Keith before we go home," Joe suggested, and they went inside to telephone.

"Too bad Marr got away," the agent said when

Frank told him about their recent adventure. "But I'm glad you and your brother are safe."

Frank drew a notebook from his pocket and opened it. "I have the registration number of the getaway plane."

"Good!" Keith said. "Let's have it. I'll check it out with the Federal Aviation Agency."

Frank gave it and hung up. The boys went to the parking lot. In a moment Frank frowned. "I thought I left our car here."

"You did," Joe said with a sinking feeling. "It—it's been stolen!"

The Hardys were momentarily paralyzed. Not only their fine convertible, but also Mr Wright's highly secret invention was gone!

Frank spoke first. "Come on, Joe! We must call the police."

The boys ran to the administration building and telephoned. They were told by the sergeant on duty that state troopers had picked up a car fitting the convertible's description. "Will you Hardys go out to the end of Pleasantdale Road and look at it?" the officer requested.

Frank hailed a taxi which took them to the spot, then back to Bayport. The convertible was a sorry sight. Every bit of the upholstery had been slashed and the contents dumped out. Articles had been removed from the front compartment and the boot. The spare tyre had been ripped open.

"Too bad, fellows," a trooper said.

"Yes," Frank answered, testing the rack.

It was still bolted in place, but he winked at Joe, a

signal that he wanted to be alone for a further search. On a pretext Joe got the trooper round to the front of the car. Quickly Frank looked under the tyre well. The box and invention were still there.

Frank slammed the lid shut. He called out, "Joe, if this baby still runs, let's go home."

The engine started promptly and the steering mechanism was undamaged. Frank signed a paper for the police, saying he was the owner of the car, then the boys rode off. As soon as they reached home, Joe carried the invention to the boys' room and hid it.

"I'm afraid that next time the gang's going to find this," he told his brother.

"I agree," Frank answered. "What do you say we ask Mother to put it in her safe-deposit box? I'm sure Dad would agree."

Mrs Hardy and Aunt Gertrude approved this idea and as soon as the bank was open the next morning, took the invention downtown. A little later the phone rang. Mrs Hardy was calling to assure her sons of its safety.

A few moments later Agent Keith telephoned. "We've lost Marr again," he said. "The FAA looked up the registration number of his plane. It belongs to a fixed base operator at a small airport in Connecticut. Marr's pilot rented the plane for the day."

"Did the owner see the pilot's flying licence?" Frank inquired.

"Yes," Keith replied. "The name listed was Harold Clark. It's a forgery! Such a licence was never issued!"

"What about the plane?"

"It was returned some time last night. The owner found it tied down on his ramp when he went to the airport early this morning."

The Hardys were downcast by the situation. Marr had vanished and they did not have the slightest lead on him. Furthermore, their car was a wreck. They reported the damage to the insurance company and waited for an investigator to come.

"We'll have to rent a car while ours is being repaired," Frank said.

He made the arrangements by phone and within half an hour a car stood in the driveway.

The boys had just sat down to lunch in the dining room when the telephone rang. Aunt Gertrude went to the kitchen to take the call.

"Yes, they're at home," the others heard her say. Presently she darted into the room. "It's about Mr Bickford!" she said quietly.

·18·

Outsmarting the Enemy

MRS HARDY and her sons lowered their eyes. They were sure Aunt Gertrude was about to announce that the kindly jeweller had died because of Marr's beating.

"Mr Bickford is—is—?" Frank asked.

"He wants to see you at the hospital," his aunt replied.

"Then he's alive!" Joe exclaimed.

"Of course he's alive," Aunt Gertrude said. "Very weak naturally, so I don't think you boys should stay long."

"When are we to go?" Frank asked.

"Mr Bickford got permission for you to come any time. He has something urgent to tell you."

Curious as to why they were being summoned, Frank and Joe left immediately to see the elderly man. Mr Bickford was partially propped up in bed. He looked ill, but he gave his visitors a warm smile.

"I'm so glad you came," he said in a voice barely above a whisper. "The doctor said a ten-minute visit so I'll get right down to business. Sit down, please. I feel it my duty to warn you boys."

"Warn us?" Frank asked. "About what?"

"That assistant who slugged me and his pals are determined to get you," Bickford answered. "Stokeley thought he was in the shop alone, but I came in the back door quietly. He was talking on the phone and seemed to be giving orders."

Mr Bickford stopped speaking and closed his eyes. He began to gasp a little. Frank jumped up and pressed a cup of ice water to the man's lips. Mr Bickford sipped it gratefully.

"Perhaps we should go," Frank suggested.

"No, no, not yet. This won't take long," Mr Bickford insisted, opening his eyes again. "I must tell you. Stokely was saying, 'Don't tell me you couldn't help your stupid mistakes. Just don't make any more! I want the Hardys on the whaler.'

"Just then Stokeley caught sight of me and hung up the phone. He turned livid, and before I could defend myself, he punched me, kicked, hit me with a stool, and acted like a crazy man. I blacked out and wakened up here." He closed his eyes and shuddered a little.

Frank and Joe stood up, sensing that Mr Bickford was exhausted and had told all he knew.

"Thanks a lot," Frank said. "Joe and I are certainly sorry we were the cause of the attack on you."

"And we'll profit from your warning, you can bet," Joe added. "Now take care of yourself."

When Frank and Joe reached home, they at once told their mother and aunt about Mr Bickford's report. "So you see, Aunt Gertrude," said Joe, "that man Chris wasn't calling you an old whaler. He was talking about trying to get us boys on their motor whaler."

"Hmm!" said Aunt Gertrude. "Well, just the same he has very bad manners. Doesn't know how to treat a lady."

Mrs Hardy was extremely concerned and said so. "I believe if Joe hadn't been rescued from that cave, those dreadful men would have put him aboard the whaler and taken him far away. Frank would have been next."

"Exactly," said Aunt Gertrude, "and I'm sure your father never intended you boys to become so deeply involved in this horrible case. I believe my brother would thank you, Laura, to forbid these boys from any further detective work against such men as Taffy Marr."

Frank and Joe were fearful their mother might take Aunt Gertrude's advice. After several moments of silence, Mrs Hardy answered. "Fenton expects his sons to follow through and see justice done. He doesn't want me to pamper them into being cowards. However," she added, "I expect them to be cautious and alert. Frank and Joe don't deliberately run into trouble."

The boys were relieved. Each kissed their mother and thanked her for her confidence. Now that the tension was over, Joe grinned and said, "Mother, we should have been born with extra eyes in the back of our heads, so that we could see in all directions."

"You could wear those special spectacles that reflect what's at the back of you," Aunt Gertrude suggested.

"But they don't work at night," Joe replied, "and that's when most of the sluggings take place."

The conversation was interrupted by the doorbell. Frank answered and was handed a special-delivery letter.

"It's for you, Mother. From Dad," he called.

Mrs Hardy opened the envelope quickly. Presently she said, "Good! Your father's coming home. That will solve a lot of problems."

She read further. "But not right away. He and Mr Wright have to testify against two men suspected of stealing the antique plane."

"Dad found it?" Joe burst out.

"Yes. Listen to this: 'I have good reason to believe the hijackers are part of the gang I've warned the boys about. I'm sure these men have pals who are watching me, tapping my phone, and intercepting radio messages, so I decided to use the mail. In an emergency you can contact me care of Elmer Hunt, president of the Oceanic Electronic Company, San Francisco.'" The rest of the note was for her personally.

Frank and Joe went upstairs and discussed their next move. Both agreed they should do everything possible to learn where the whaler was moored.

"I guess it wouldn't be too smart to use our *Sleuth* to hunt down the whaler," Frank remarked. "We'd be spotted in a moment. And anyway we haven't fixed the horn yet."

"I don't think it'd be good to take Tony's boat, either," Joe said. He was referring to their school friend Tony Prito.

"How about arranging with somebody who has a cabin cruiser to help us make a search?" Frank suggested.

Joe's eyes twinkled. "Pretty expensive. How about the tug that nearly rammed you in the fog. Was there a name on it?"

"I'm not sure, Joe. I was pretty busy getting out of the

way! But I think I saw the word *Annie* on the side."

The boys decided to go to the docks on their motor-cycles. These were easier to manœuvre and hide than their rented car.

Soon after they left, Frank and Joe noticed that a car with three men in it was following them. None of the passengers looked familiar.

"We'd better do something fast and shake off those men!" Frank advised.

"Guess we'll have to play *hare and hounds*," Joe observed. "What do you suggest?"

"Head for Biff Hooper's and pretend to be staying there," Frank answered. "We can sneak out of their back door before those men have a chance to go round to the garden."

Joe nodded. "And take a back street to the docks. Score one for us!"

They explained their plan to Mrs Hooper, who let them out of the kitchen door. Frank and Joe hurriedly crossed the back lawn, which was out of sight of the street. They jumped the hedge. Twenty minutes later the Hardys were in Harbour Master Crogan's office inquiring about a tugboat named *Annie*.

The man flipped open a large ledger and ran down a list. "I guess you mean the *Annie K*. She comes in here once in a while."

"Is she docked now?" Joe asked.

"I'll see." Crogan consulted a chart on the wall. "Yes, she is. Waiting for some kind of shipment that's been delayed."

Frank and Joe glanced at each other. There might be a chance of chartering the tug!

"Does the captain own the *Annie K?*" Frank inquired.

"Yes, and a real nice man he is too. Name's Captain Volper."

The Hardys got directions on where to find the tugboat, thanked Crogan, and left. Captain Volper was seated cross-legged on the deck of the *Annie K*, reading the morning paper. He was a ruddy-complexioned, slightly plump, good-natured man.

"Howdy, boys!" he greeted the brothers. "And what can I do for you?"

Frank made their request.

"So you want to take a cruise round the bay, up and down the coast, eh? Well, I guess I could do it." He laughed. "You fellows got some money with you?"

"Sure thing," Frank replied. "Can we cast off now?"

"Soon's I can get my crew out o' the coffee shop across the street."

He ambled off down the gangplank and was gone nearly fifteen minutes while the boys walked up and down impatiently. Then Volper returned with two sailors, whom he introduced as Hank and Marcy.

A few minutes later the old tugboat pulled away from the dock. The boys decided to stay in the cabin so as not to be seen by anyone going past in other boats.

"Captain Volper, did you ever notice a motor whaler around here?" Frank asked.

"Yes, about two weeks ago. Then I got caught in the fog and plumb near run somebody down." Frank and Joe glanced at each other.

"Does the whaler have a name on it?" Joe asked.

The captain tilted back his cap and scratched his

head. "Seems to me it did. That's harbour regulations, you know. Let me see now." Unable to recall the name he summoned Hank and Marcy and asked them.

"Sure I remember it," Marcy replied. "Man alive, I wish I could own one o' them plastic boats. They got speed. The name o' this one I seen anchored up near the caves was *Water Devil*."

"I'll bet it is, too," Joe commented, but did not explain the double meaning in his remark.

The tug went directly to the spot and the boys gazed at the sleek whaler, which was anchored in shallow water. No one seemed to be around.

"Ship ahoy!" Volper shouted. There was no answer.

"I'm going aboard," Frank announced. When the captain reminded him that the law dealt harshly with snoopers, the young detective said, "Did you know smugglers are operating in this territory?"

Volper and his crew were amazed.

"And you think this is their boat?" the captain asked.

"We suspect so," Frank replied. "We'd like to go aboard and hunt for clues."

The captain sighed. "Boys today are too smart for me. Go ahead."

He pulled up close to the whaler and the Hardys jumped down on to the deck of the *Water Devil*. At first they made a casual surveillance. Seeing nothing suspicious, the boys began opening lockers.

"This is the gang's boat all right," Joe sang out, holding up a piece of paper with red and blue stripes on it. A few figures had been scrawled on it.

"Say, Frank, do you suppose there are any diamonds or electronic equipment hidden aboard?"

"Let's look!"

Nothing came to light until they opened a dashboard compartment. A sack lay inside. Both boys reached for it at once. The next second they were hurled violently across the deck. They blacked out and toppled into the water.

Anchor Pete

On the deck of the *Annie K*, Captain Volper and his crewmen stood stunned by the sudden accident. But not for long. Instantly Hank and Marcy jumped into the water.

"I'll get this one," Hank called, indicating Joe as the boy's limp form bobbed to the surface.

Marcy set off with fast strokes to rescue Frank. In less than a minute the two Hardys were lying on the deck of the tugboat and being given first aid. They did not respond.

"We'd better get these boys to the hospital as soon as possible," Captain Volper said worriedly.

He set the ship's engines to maximum capacity and sent a radio message for an ambulance to meet him at the dock. By the time Frank and Joe regained consciousness, they were in a Bayport Hospital room and Dr Bates was there, as well as Mrs Hardy and Aunt Gertrude.

Relief spread across the watchers' faces as the boys managed wan smiles. "I guess we gave you all a good scare," Joe remarked. "Say, where are we?"

When the boys were told, Frank said, "Joe and I must have been *out* a long time. I remember we touched a sack in that whaler and then—wham! What happened to us?"

"You fellows got a bad electric shock," Dr Bates explained, "and were thrown into the water. If Captain Volper hadn't been there, you would have drowned. Hank and Marcy rescued you."

"Thank goodness," Mrs Hardy murmured.

"The person who rigged up that device got a shock of his own," Aunt Gertrude said crisply, "and I'm glad he did."

"He was caught?" Joe asked. "Who is he?"

"Your kidnapper—at least this is what the police think from your description of him," Aunt Gertrude said. "When you feel well enough, you're to go down to headquarters and identify this man you call Gross."

"How was he captured?" Joe asked impatiently.

The boys sat open-mouthed in astonishment as they listened. Captain Volper had notified the Coast Guard and the Harbour Police. Both had gone out at once to the spot where the *Water Devil* was moored. Nothing had been disturbed and the men were sure no one would show up until the launches moved away.

"The police decided to leave a couple of their skin divers to watch," Dr Bates told Frank and Joe. "Soon after the others had left, a rowing-boat came from shore. The man in it boarded the whaler. He looked worried at seeing the compartment open, but seemed relieved that the sack was still there. He clicked off a switch, then picked up the sack with no harm to himself. As he reboarded the rowing-boat with it, the man was overpowered by the two skin divers."

"What was in the sack?" Joe queried.

"Exactly what you might expect," Aunt Gertrude said. "Diamonds and valuable electronic equipment."

Mrs Hardy told her sons that both the *Water Devil* and the rowing-boat had been impounded by the authorities and were being examined for further clues since the prisoner would reveal nothing.

Joe wanted to go right down to headquarters and see the man, but Dr Bates forbade this.

"May I call Chief Collig?" Joe asked.

A phone was brought to the room and plugged in. Soon Joe was talking to the chief, who was amazed and delighted that the Hardys had recovered.

"I want to see the prisoner," Joe told him. "Dr Bates says I can't come down. Could you possibly bring him here?"

The others in the room gasped at the request, but Dr Bates nodded his approval after the chief had said, "If the doctor thinks it's okay." The physician left but Mrs Hardy and Aunt Gertrude remained.

Twenty minutes later the prisoner arrived with two officers, one of them with a tape recorder already turned on.

"He's Gross all right!" Joe burst out. "My kidnapper!"

The man was sullen. He murmured defiantly, "You can't prove a thing."

"Proof?" Joe scoffed. "I heard plenty in the cave. And somebody else besides me got a look at you when you were snooping in our car." He did not mention Iola's name.

When Gross made no answer, Aunt Gertrude cried out, "You ought to be horsewhipped! Jail's too good for people like you. Kidnapper, smuggler, and goodness knows what else!"

As she paused to take a deep breath, Frank spoke up. "Gross, you tried to starve my brother and you doped him."

The prisoner finally began to talk. "I—I had to do what I was told or risk being killed myself."

"You mean by Taffy Marr?" Frank shot at him.

Gross winced. "Yes. I shouldn't tell you, but it don't matter now. I got nothing to lose. Marr takes away every diamond and electronic gadget we steal and smuggle in and threatens us besides. I'm better off in jail."

One of the officers remarked, "Things will go a lot better for you if you tell everything. Where is Marr now?"

"I don't know. He was watching me from the shore with binoculars. When I got caught I'm sure he ducked into hiding. That's the way he does. When things get too hot, every man for himself. Then in one month we meet up again."

"What's the next place?" the officer asked.

"Portland, Maine."

"No plans until then?"

Several seconds passed before Gross answered. Finally he said, "Each man was ordered to get the Hardy boys one way or another. Maybe some of 'em will stay around here and try it."

"Oh, I hope not!" Mrs Hardy exclaimed.

Frank asked the prisoner, "Who do you think will get after us first? And where?"

Gross did not answer directly. "I don't want to see

you guys get hurt, but I can't help you. Chris might decide to stick around, or Anchor Pete."

"Anchor Pete?" Joe repeated.

"Yeah—he's a sailor and a smuggler. Used to pitch an anchor like you'd pitch horseshoes and he'd bet he could throw one farther'n anybody else. He could, too. You guys had better watch out."

Gross, who finally said his first name was John, had no record. Marr had saved him from being beaten up by a gang, so Gross had felt indebted to him. "But I was wrong. He made a no-good out o' me. And what do I get? Jail!"

The bitter prisoner was led away. A nurse came in with food for the boys and announced that as soon as they had eaten they were to go to sleep.

Mrs Hardy and Aunt Gertrude kissed Frank and Joe good night and left. As the boys ate, they discussed the latest developments in the case and how they should tackle them when they resumed their detective work.

"I have an idea," Frank said. "How about asking Chet and Biff and Jerry to shadow us while we let ourselves be seen around?"

Joe grinned. "Hoping to be attacked, you mean?"

"Right." Frank thought it doubtful that this would occur in daylight. "We'll reverse our schedule—sleep in the daytime and roam at night."

From his bed Joe shook hands with himself, indicating, "Agreed."

Three days went by before Dr Bates told the boys they were as good as new. "And stay that way!" he advised with a meaningful laugh.

Meanwhile, Frank and Joe had arranged with their friends to carry out the sleuthing programme.

"Okay," said Chet, "but I think your scheme is pretty risky. Taffy Marr may have shadows following his men and they could be behind the other fellows and me."

"We'll just have to take that chance," Biff had said.

The first night was spent along the waterfront where the Hardys were sure Anchor Pete would be stationed. Frank and Joe walked together at times, then would separate. They deliberately went into dark areas and deserted spots. No one bothered them and later their friends reported having seen nothing suspicious.

"Tomorrow night," said Frank as the group separated, "we'll try the high school and athletic grounds and football stadium."

Again the boys were not disturbed and so far as they could judge were not followed.

"What's next?" Biff asked.

Joe felt that perhaps Marr's gang had learned the Hardys' friends were helping them and suggested he and Frank try the sleuthing alone.

"Nothing doing," Chet spoke up.

It was decided that the third night would be spent in the heart of town and would last only until just before midnight. It rained, but once more Frank and Joe led the way through dark streets and up and down deserted alleys. Finally, at ten minutes to twelve, they heard Biff whistle, Jerry give the sound of a hoot owl, and Chet yap like a dog.

"Quitting time," Frank remarked.

"Yes," Joe said. "Three nights of walking and not

one thing happening. By this time Marr and the rest of his gang could be halfway round the world."

Frank sighed from weariness and disappointment. "Let's take a short cut across the square."

They headed for the small park which lay in the centre of Bayport. Various municipal buildings, including the town hall with its large illuminated clock, outlined the four sides.

Frank and Joe reached the square and took a diagonal path through it. The place seemed empty. Part way across, Joe suddenly said, "I just saw someone dodge behind that big tree ahead."

"We'd better wait," Frank answered.

The Hardys jumped at the back of a wide-trunked maple. When no one ventured towards them, the boys peered out, looking in opposite directions for a possible attacker. Seconds later there was a shuffling sound behind them.

"Look out!" a voice yelled.

Frank and Joe turned in time to see a masked sailor swinging a heavy anchor. He was about to crash it on Frank's head!

·20·

Captives' Hideout

THE sailor's diabolical move was accompanied by the midnight striking of the clock, shouts from all directions, and a prolonged war whoop that could come from no one but Chet Morton. As Frank and Joe dodged the anchor, footsteps pounded in their direction.

The boys grabbed the sailor and held him tightly. In a moment Chet, Biff, Jerry, and Mr Hardy rushed up.

"Dad!" his sons cried. "When did you get home?"

"I haven't been home yet," the detective answered. "Came from the airport and dropped off Mr Wright. As I rode past here, Chet hailed me."

Frank stared at the other boys and said, "I thought you'd gone."

"What do you take us for?" Chet asked. "Did you think we'd run out on you? We were planning to follow you to your house."

All this time the sailor was wriggling, trying to break away from his captors.

Joe looked at him hard. "Hold still, Anchor Pete." he ordered. "You'll stay right here until the police come for you."

"And his pal," Biff put in. "I kayoed him back by that tree."

The sailor's jaw dropped. "Ben?" he said unbelievingly. "And you know my name too?"

"Sure," Frank answered. "Your buddy Gross squealed."

Meanwhile, Mr Hardy had pulled his two-way short-wave set from a pocket and began talking to police headquarters. He told what had happened and asked that Keith and Mallett of the FBI be notified. The sergeant agreed and said he would send a squad car and four men to the park immediately.

While waiting, Frank and Joe asked the other boys to hold the captive sailor so that they could take a look at Biff's victim. When Joe beamed his flashlight on the man's face, he exclaimed, "This guy was in the cave with my kidnapper!"

The boys dragged the man back to where Anchor Pete was standing. The sight made the sailor blanch and the Hardys figured that maybe he was so frightened he might talk if quizzed.

"Pete, the game's up!" Frank said. "You can tell us about Taffy Marr now."

The sailor squinted his eyes and looked into space, as if trying to make up his mind what he should do. At last he said, "I'll talk. Marr's gone to make a pickup."

"Diamonds? Electronic parts?" Joe asked.

"Yeah."

"Where?"

"Along the bay. Maybe near the caves."

At that moment the police car arrived and the two prisoners were put inside. Before the driver pulled away, he said to the Hardys, "Sergeant asked me to give you a message. Keith and his assistant Mallet are already in town. They're at your house."

The Hardys said goodnight to Chet, Biff, and Jerry, thanking them for their fine work.

"Any time," the three responded.

On their way home Frank and Joe asked their father how he had learned about the gang. "I got a tip from a detective friend in Chicago, but he wasn't sure just which gang it was."

When the three reached home they found Mrs Hardy and Aunt Gertrude with the two FBI agents. They had already briefed the men on the latest developments in the case.

"Our night's work isn't finished," Frank spoke up. "We have a new lead to Taffy Marr."

"We'll go right after him," Keith said.

"As soon as we put on dry clothes and get raincoats," Mr Hardy said.

Within ten minutes the five were ready to leave the house. Mr Hardy drove his car. The gentle rain had now changed to a severe storm. Thunder boomed and vivid flashes of lightning streaked down from the black sky.

When the Hardys and the two agents reached the area of the caves, the detective parked and the searchers groped their way down the hillside.

"There's a narrow path between the cliffs just ahead," Frank told the others. "It leads directly down to the water."

He led the way to the path and started down it. The teeming rain made the footing treacherous. Occasionally a flash of lightning illuminated the entire hillside, forcing the sleuths to crouch low to avoid detection.

During one of the flashes, Joe pointed to the shore below. "I saw a man standing down there! He could be Marr!"

The searchers continued to stalk their way along the steep path. When they were a little more than halfway to the bottom, Mr Hardy signalled for his companions to stop.

"Keith, how about our sitting here for a while and seeing what that man is up to," Mr Hardy whispered. "This spot is a good vantage point, and there are enough bushes to provide cover."

"Good idea."

As they watched the shore below, the watchers suddenly saw a flashlight beam flicker on and off several times.

"Marr must be signalling to someone," Mallet said.

"What's that?" Keith snapped, pointing off into the distance.

There had been an answering gleam from far out in the bay. The light flashed once, twice, then out completely.

A few minutes later there was a flash of lightning that bathed the entire area in a blue-white glare. In that moment the boys and their companions caught a glimpse of a small rowing-boat making its way inshore across the choppy waters.

"Did you see that?" Frank cried. "Four men in that boat."

"Let's go down for a closer look," Joe suggested.

They descended cautiously, edging their way through

the bushes towards the spot where the man was standing. Through the storm they heard a faint shout. Again the suspect signalled with his flashlight. He was guiding the boat inland.

As it drew closer, the sleuths heard the rattle of oarlocks. They crept a bit nearer and, about forty feet away, they could clearly distinguish the waiting figure near the water's edge.

The gang-leader switched on his flashlight again. The rowing-boat was approaching. It rocked to and fro, its bow high in the water.

"That you, Marr?" someone called.

"Yes, but shut up!"

At last they were going to confront Marr!

"We can't risk letting those men get away," Keith muttered. "When the boat lands, we'll arrest them!"

The agents drew their pistols. With Mr Hardy they poised for action. The detective ordered his sons to step back.

The rowing-boat was now in shallow water. Two of the occupants leaped out and pushed the craft on to the beach.

"This is it!" Keith declared. "Let's go!"

He sprang from the bushes with Mallett and Mr Hardy.

"Put up your hands!" the agent shouted. "And don't make a move!"

There was a yell from the dim figures on the beach. One of the men was about to push the rowing-boat back into deep water when Mallet fired two shots over his head.

As the agents ran towards the suspects, Frank caught

sight of a man running off down the beach and he raced after him. Behind him he could hear shouts, another shot, then the sounds of a struggle.

The fleeing man plunged on into the darkness, but the young detective overtook him quickly. His quarry suddenly turned, crouched low, and as Frank came up he lashed out with his fists.

The boy dodged the blow, then grappled with the man. A clenched fist struck the young sleuth in the face and sent him sprawling.

Frank recovered instantly and scrambled to his feet. His opponent turned and fled. Again Frank overtook him and brought the man down with a flying tackle. In a tight clinch they rolled across the beach and into shallow water. Finally Frank managed to get in a blow that knocked his opponent unconscious. He dragged him out of the water.

Joe, meanwhile, had plunged knee-deep into the water and grabbed a man who was trying to haul the boat away from shore. They lashed out at each other. Joe was knocked down. He struggled to his feet, choking and gasping, and followed his tall, muscular opponent on to the beach. The man aimed a blow, but Joe side-stepped it, then rushed in and drove his fists into the other's body. The gangster grunted and doubled up with pain.

Joe noticed that Mallet was sprawled on the ground apparently unconscious and that Mr Hardy and Keith were still battling two men.

Joe suddenly realized that Taffy Marr had escaped and was now rowing off in a sheet of rain.

"Marr is getting away!" he shouted.

"What!" Keith yelled. "And we don't have a boat to go after him!" He fired a shot in the air, but the suspect did not halt.

Mallet recovered and got to his feet just as Frank arrived, shoving his prisoner ahead of him.

"Marr escaped in the rowing-boat!" Joe told his brother, and picked up the flashlight Marr had dropped. He directed its beam on the prisoners.

"I recognize three of these guys!" he exclaimed as Keith and Mallet handcuffed the men. "They visited Chris in the cave when I was there."

They were searched and bags of diamonds and small electronic equipment were removed from their pockets.

"Where'd you get these?" Mr Hardy asked.

"They're legit," one man said.

"We know you're smugglers," the detective said, "and we can trace these."

"Okay. They were dropped to us off a ship. In this storm I didn't see the name of it."

"Where's Marr going?" Frank asked one prisoner.

"You're not gettin' anything more out of us!"

"That's not being smart," Keith said. "After all, Marr left you behind to face the music. It might help you get off with lighter sentences if you co-operate." Silence.

"Why don't you tell us what you know?" Frank queried.

"I—I want to," the man stammered. "But I'm afraid of—of the boss."

"You mean Marr? Where is he?"

"I guess up on the north shore of Barmet Bay. Place

called Rocky Point. Marr had me rent an old shack there. He uses it as a hideout."

"Where's Chris?" Joe questioned.

"Probably waiting for Marr."

Mr Hardy radioed Bayport Police Headquarters again and told them that they had captured more of the smugglers. The sergeant promised to notify the Harbour Police to pick them up.

"I hope they come soon," Joe said. "We must go after Marr before he skips."

The launch arrived in an incredibly short time and the prisoners were handed over. Then Frank said to the captain, "We may need you again soon. Up at Rocky Point."

"Let us know," the skipper said and chugged off.

The Hardys and the FBI agents climbed the cliff, then rode along Shore Road to Rocky Point. In this area the bluff was not as steep and the sleuths had no trouble descending it. They were just in time to see a man with a lantern meeting an arriving rowing-boat.

"That's Chris!" Frank whispered.

"And Marr," Joe added. "Let's rush 'em!"

"Not yet," Keith said. "I have a tape recorder in my pocket. We may find their conversation useful."

As Keith had hoped, the two smugglers talked freely.

"I guess we can now clear out of Bayport for good," Marr said. "Chris, when we get to Portland, you set up a whole new gang. Make friends with the crew of a new ship and pick out one like Beef Danion on the *Rizzolo*. Too bad we have to chuck him."

"But, Taffy," said Chris, "you goin' to leave here without getting Wright's secret radio? You said that if you used that, nobody could ever catch us. It would scramble messages among the gang and from ship to shore. And the dicks couldn't interfere, or a bad storm stop your orders from reaching us."

"I know," Marr answered, "but right now our skin's more important. Maybe I shouldn't have hung around after I slugged Bickford. But I needed tonight's haul."

"What about your stealin' Wright's antique plane?" Chris asked.

Marr gave a sardonic laugh. "It served its purpose— kept Mr Wright and Mr Hardy away from here. But those kids, Frank and Joe, are pests. All the Hardys are too clever."

The boys were smiling. Marr did not know that one of the secret radios was hidden in Wright's plane, and now it had been recovered!

By this time Marr and Chris had reached the one-room shack and went inside. Again the boys wanted to rush the place, but their father held them back.

"You watch through that window," he ordered.

Going off a little distance, the detective radioed the Harbour Police.

Then he and the FBI men got ready to burst open the unlocked door. Inside, the smugglers were busily packing suitcases. They had stopped talking.

At a signal Keith opened the door and dashed into the room with Mallett and Mr Hardy. Taken by surprise, Marr and Chris had no chance to put up any resistance and were handcuffed to await the Harbour Police. When Frank and Joe came in, they received looks of furious resentment from the prisoners.

Meanwhile, the smugglers' suitcases were examined.

Many secret pockets and a false bottom were found, each containing a fabulous quantity of jewels and electronic equipment.

Joe broke the silence. "Wowee, these smugglers could have retired rich!" he remarked.

Presently the police arrived and the two men were taken away. Keith and Mallett went with them. As the launch departed, Frank and Joe realized that another mystery had also departed. They were to experience a "lost" feeling until their next case, *The Sinister Signpost*, came along.

On the way home, the boys and their father filled in the gaps of the present mystery. "Mr Wright is very pleased with your work," said Mr Hardy, "but he's ready to sell his antique plane."

"We know who will buy it," Joe spoke up. "Cole Weber."

"What about the special radio, Dad?" Frank asked. "Surely there's more to it than what we know."

Mr Hardy chuckled. He did not answer directly and they guessed the secret was a highly classified one. Instead, he said, "Some day how would you boys like to own pocket radios that can pick up signals from outer space?"

"You mean that's what Mr Wright has done?" Joe cried out.

The detective gave his sons a broad wink.

Have you seen
the Hardy Boys
lately?

Now you can continue to enjoy the Hardy Boys in a new action-packed series written especially for older readers. Each book has more high-tech adventure, intrigue, mystery and danger than ever before.

Join Frank and Joe in these fabulous adventures, available only in Armada.

1	Dead on Target	£2.25	☐
2	Evil, Incorporated	£2.25	☐
3	Cult of Crime	£2.25	☐
4	The Lazarus Plot	£2.25	☐

ARMADA

All these books are available at your local bookshop or newsagent, or can be ordered from the publisher. To order direct from the publishers just tick the title you want and fill in the form below:

Name _____

Address _____

_____

Send to: Collins Childrens Cash Sales
            PO Box 11
            Falmouth
            Cornwall
            TR10 9EN

Please enclose a cheque or postal order or debit my Visa/ Access –

Credit card no:

Expiry date:

Signature:

– to the value of the cover price plus:

UK: 60p for the first book, 25p for the second book, plus 15p per copy for each additional book ordered to a maximum charge of £1.90.

BFPO: 60p for the first book, 25p for the second book plus 15p per copy for the next 7 books, thereafter 9p per book.

Overseas and Eire: £1.25 for the first book, 75p for the second book. Thereafter 28p per book.

Armada reserve the right to show new retail prices on covers which may differ from those previously advertised in the text or elsewhere.

ARMADA